HELEN'S

DAIMONES

BY

S. E. LINDBERG

HELEN'S DAIMONES

DYSCRASIA FICTION®

S.E. LINDBERG

Helen's Daimones
Copyright © 2017 by S. E. Lindberg
ISBN-10:0-9838262-5-0
ISBN-13:978-0-9838262-5-5

Dyscrasia Fiction ® is a registered trademark of IGNIS Publishing LLC, 8064 Seabury Court, West Chester, OH 45069

The Morpheus Font is used with permission from Kiwi Media.

Front Cover Art © 2016 Daniel Landerman
Cover Design by S. E. Lindberg and H. L. Lindberg
Edited by Forrest Aguirre

Other Works by S.E. Lindberg

IGNIS Publishing LLC's Dyscrasia Fiction®
Listed in story chronology:

- 2011 *Lords of Dyscrasia*
- 2017 *Helen's Daimones*
- 2014 *Spawn of Dyscrasia*
- *Helen's Storm* (working title)

Perseid Press contributions:

- 2015, "Legacy of the Great Dragon" story in *Heroika 1: Dragon Eaters* anthology
- 2017, "Curse of the Pharaohs" story in *Pirates in Hell, a Heroes in Hell* anthology
- "The Naked Daemon" story accepted for *Heroika 2: Shieldless/Skirmishers*

Praise For Dyscrasia Fiction

Black Gate Magazine raves: "Lindberg is the real deal, a gifted writer with a strong command of language, and a soaring talent that stretches beyond the verbal: he illustrates his novel with his own wild and weird and excellent drawings. If you like action-packed dark fantasy with bizarre settings, an original premise and clever twist, then add [Lords of Dyscrasia] to your Must Read List." — *Author Joe Bonadonna, 2015*

Foreword Clarion, 5/5 Stars: "…highly recommended, though not for the faint of heart…Outside of the works of Poe and Lovecraft, there are few, if any, novels comparable to [Lords of Dyscrasia]. It has a bardic tone, as if it was a tale told over many nights. Beowulf comes to mind both for its epic quality and bloody action… the pace is nearly breathless…""… makes the majority of current popular fantasy fiction read like recipes…" — *Reviewer Janine Stinson 2011*

"I'm impressed. [Spawn of Dyscrasia] is an entertaining fantasy novel that—I would argue—rises to the level of art. I judge that in a couple of ways. First, the actual prose here is simply lovely. It has the kind of poetry and descriptiveness to it that I constantly seek for but seldom find. Note: by lovely I don't mean that it is sweet and bucolic. Quite the reverse. There are plenty of gore-rich scenes, enough to do a horror novel proud. But the language is so vivid and rich that you can just revel in it." — *Author Charles Gramlich, 2014*

Beauty in Ruins Book Reviews: "[Spawn of Dyscrasia is] very well-constructed, with an interesting system of magic to drive the plot forward, but it's hardly what one would call your typical heroic, uplifting fantasy. In fact, it's as much a horror novel as it is a fantasy novel, but it's in that clash of genres that Lindberg distinguishes himself. This reads very much like an epic fantasy novel in terms of language and imagery, but one dealing with a dark, gruesome, horrific sort of subject matter. It's a gorgeous, textured, intricately layered story where every word counts, and where no phrase is wasted. Make no mistake, it makes for heavy reading, but you feel the weight of every word." — *Reviewer Bob Milne, 2014*

Horror Author Review: "I am no stranger to Dark Fantasy. I first discovered it as a kid and continued discovering more throughout life. Some of it stands out from the rest. Clark Ashton's Smith's work does. Some of H.P. Lovecraft's does. William Hope Hodgson's NIGHT LAND and HOUSE ON THE BORDERLAND does. Much of Edgar Allen Poe's does. And S.E. Lindberg does. However, although there are haunting echoes in Lindberg's Dyscrasia tales that reflect the works of those other legendary Dark Fantasy storytellers, the addition of fine artwork throughout SPAWN OF DYSCRASIA and even more so LORDS OF DYSCRASIA push this work, for me, into another realm of reader's heaven and leads me to find only one other writer who created such a complex and unique world, Mervyn Peake. The Ghormenghast creation that is Peake's crowning achievement has never been equaled, in my opinion. Lindberg's Dyscrasia has not been equaled either and is unlikely to be. The world of the Dyscrasia stories is not one any sane person would WANT to live in, but if you are like me, once there, you may not want to leave." — *C. Dean Andersson, 2014*

"Know yourself. Once again, that expression provides the subtle undertone that permeates the life-threads of our protagonists in the decades following the ending of the Ill Age, where Dyscrasia was vanquished…. I have to say that, once again, I was captivated by the wonderful blend of high action and deep, meaningful – almost poetic prose – that Lindberg manages to weave throughout his narrative. It is an extremely engaging tale, and one I thoroughly enjoyed. I really would recommend you take the time to discover more about the land ruled by Dyscrasia, as it is one of the most evocative empyreal worlds you will ever enter." — *Best Selling Author of IX, Andrew Paul Weston 2017*

DYSCRASIA FICTION

DYSCRASIA FICTION® EXPLORES the choices humans and their gods make as a disease corrupts their souls, shared blood, and creative energies. Literally, dyscrasia means "a bad mixture of liquids" (it is not a magical land). Historically, dyscrasia referred to any imbalance of the four medicinal humors professed by the ancient Greeks to sustain life (phlegm, blood, black & yellow bile). Artisans, anatomists, and chemists of the Renaissance evolved humorism to include aspects of alchemical elements (water, air, earth, and fire) and psychological temperaments (phlegmatic, sanguine, melancholic, and choleric). In short, the humors are mystical media of color, energy, and emotion; *Dyscrasia Fiction*® presents them as spiritual muses for artisans, sources of magical power, and contagions of a deadly disease.

Map

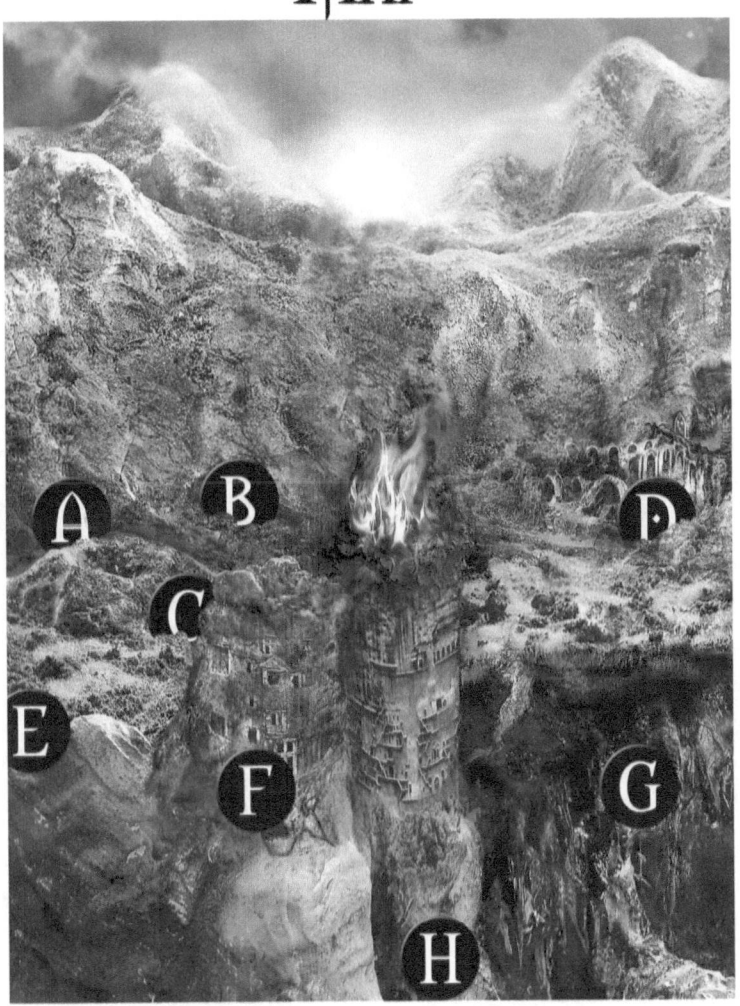

A: Cypria's Gallwomb
B: Clan Qual
C: Gorgepath
D: Clan Tonn

E: To Clan Lysis
F: Chromlchon Keep
   & Pyre
G: Blood Bogs
H: Underworld

Acknowledgements

Undying thanks to Team Lindberg:

Art Director, Heidi

Resident Mythologist, Erin

Truth Teller, Connor

Therapy Pets, Shorty & Sweetie

...and to my professional partners:

Cover Artist, Daniel Landerman

Editing Services, Forrest Aguirre

Contents

I: Girls' Play

Lithe, ivory-haired Helen crouched in the meadow. She spied the emerging fireflies, ready to play. A storm brewed on the distant, western horizon. Remote, thunderless lightning seemed to communicate to the fireflies with pulsing flashes. She wished she could interpret such magic.

"One day, I will understand your secret language," Helen vowed.

She was accustomed to being apart from people, immersed in her own reality. Cloaked in a cougar pelt splotched with green dye, she was empowered by her feline familiar's aura: Angie. She was not alone with her invisible friend. Her living cats were about too. Nearest was the piebald, Spotty, who rubbed whiskers against her grass-stained knees. Its siblings, Shadow and Smokey, and their mother, the tabby Queen-Bee, were mere feet away, preparing to pounce. Helen was only tracking the brilliant bugs—not hunting them. She fancied the fireflies as children, playing so haphazardly that they might hurt themselves. As their 'mother,' she had to gather them and bring them home. Collecting them was an impossible task, and fruitless, since she released any catch. Fun, in any event.

Nature blew a burst of wind across the highlands. This awakened the horde of fireflies, lifting them from their milkweed perches. Arisen, they flashed their chartreuse lights under the hastening sheen of twilight. Helen leaned forward, eager to give chase. The ground rumbled slightly. She paused to listen. A horse-drawn carriage approached. She smiled. Her friend had come from Qual.

O N THE WESTERN edge of the field, where a road cut through the grass, an orchid mantis took flight. It approached the travelers from behind, landing and becoming instantly motionless on Mum's back shoulder. Tiny Sharon stared in silence at its violet-rimmed eyes. Pink spikes emerged from the regal mantis. Sharon was reminded of the puffy, floral gowns adorning the manikins in Qual's Hall of Mirrors. Sunlight glared off the glossy pearl shell. Its abdomen was much larger than its waist, as if outfitted in a tournure. The presence before her was that of a cultivated lady. Perhaps it was attracted to the lavender perfume of her mother.

Sharon attempted to pretty herself. Her attire had skewed during the ride, so she readjusted her sky-blue, skirted bodice and muslin underdress. Her laced cap failed to contain her red curls, so she brushed them out of her face. She used her tongue to check on her loose, top tooth. It had just begun to wiggle.

"Stop playing with your teeth. We can take care of that when we get back home. Now sit straight," her mother said. The younger woman obeyed. "Sharon, you must remain civil when you play with your wild friend."

"In the fields, Mum?"

Nadeen's lips tightened, eyelids narrowed. "You shall *not* be leaving my side."

Lady Nadeen held her hand tighter. Echoes of oft-repeated warnings resonated in Sharon's head. Her mother need not say the litany again: *'Beware the black birds, and the wasps. They will abduct you.'* All those dangers applied anywhere. The warnings were warranted, but staying beside her mother would not make her safer, either. Sharon had witnessed servants plucked from the safety of the city's walls. Helen was a bit wild, but not in a dangerous way. Sharon looked toward her father for support. He focused on steering the horses, stealing a hasty glimpse to shrug his shoulders and wink.

Nadeen continued. "Behave like a lady. You should not go out of my sight. There are dangers out there. Worse than those back home."

The setting sun did little to slow the countryside gnats, which seemed larger than their city brethren were. Sharon held tight to her osier picnic basket and the leather arm of her doll, Lacey. She wondered if her mother would ever notice the beady-eyed mantis clinging on her stole. Mum despised insects. An hour of jostling on the wooden seat was enough to rattle her mother's nerves. Mum may overreact and crush that mantis.

The carriage stopped. Sharon's Papa dismounted, placing his brimmed hat beneath his left arm. "We have arrived, ladies." His exposed periwig swelled in the rural air as he helped his wife and daughter off the wagon. Expansive hills and the boundless landscape surrounded them. Grass reached over Sharon's head. She walked behind her Papa squeezing her doll.

"Lord Donquason, nephew of Clanlord Qualenson! I trust your uncle has returned?" The aproned furrier welcomed them with a smile, a scraper carved from bone in his hand. A vest of bear fur wrapped his barrel chest, the top of which blended seamlessly with a mottled, unkempt beard. His sweaty, exposed arms glistened.

"The clanlord's manor remains eerily empty," Donquason bowed slightly, "greetings my friend, the furrier."

"Helen's Papa?" Sharon whispered, remembering.

"You did not recognize me at first glance, my darling Sharon? Of course, I am Helen's father. She calls me 'Da' for the record." Helen's father turned his smirk into an empathetic frown as he addressed Lord Don again to inquire about dark times. "Well, then. Six months have passed, and it is good that Qual has you to lead. You'll be named official regent soon?"

Somberly, Lord Don confirmed. "Yes. I am the closest of blood. And I have the clearest plans to rejuvenate the clan. Please do not be offended if I keep you out of the manor house? That is," he laughed, "until you've had a proper bath."

"Regent Donny, if I may be so bold, I think you crave a celebratory gesture." Helen's father bear-hugged him for several seconds, lifting him into the air just long enough to ensure his friend blushed. Lady Nadeen stepped back. Her glare clarified her desire to avoid similar treatment. Sharon hid behind her. The furrier continued, "You are anxious to learn of the experiments, but I am sure Sharon would rather see Helen than listen to us. Let us find her. Come along." He led the guests.

Smoke from the homestead's stove pit and beamhouse mingled with Lady Nadeen's lavender perfume. "The air smells less foul than expected." She said, adjusting her scarf to cover her nose. At once, she froze in alarm observing the mantis. Then she shook in silence.

Sharon stayed her mother's elbow. "'tis a good bug, Mum."

Lady Nadeen shut her eyes. Then she breathed deep to reinvigorate her resolve. Her daughter was too young to remember the swarms of flesh-eating wasps that had ravaged the district of Clan Qual; they burrowed into men's eyes, mouths, and ears, possessed their minds, compelled them to wander off. Evil sorcery had taken hundreds. Tears welled as memories resurfaced.

Sharon's father brushed the mantis away cautiously. The haunting memories dispelled.

"My cauldrons do smell a bit," Helen's father continued, "but not like the urine vats closer to town. I do not have enough livestock here, nor the abundant people, to source it. But Apothecary Whitebeard supplied me with lime and lye to use as an alternative. A slurry from the Tonn quarries works well to remove hair from hide, and the materials are easier to inventory than piss."

"Does it affect the color?" Lady Nadeen brushed her gown proactively to keep away crawlers.

"I have experimented dyeing while liming. I think the lye helps. It may act as a mordant too." He handed over three leather strips. They were pliable, soft, and colored: verdigris, cerulean, turmeric.

The wigged Donquason stared wide-eyed, "You are gifted. If only Clanlord Qualenson was here to see. Regardless, the guilds will adore these."

The adults quieted to reflect on the missing clanlord. There was little they could do about Qualenson leaving with his son. Those two royals had been mesmerized by a goddess' spell. Still, the survivors must carry on. The devastated clan persevered. "Well, customers may enjoy them, until the beauty fades." Nadeen inspected the strands. "Do they hold fast to color in sunlight?"

"Too early to tell, my Lady. I'll need more of those dyestuffs if you want me to continue testing." Helen's father said. "There is still the matter of post treatment which may help seal in color, or perhaps dampen it. Many options to improve that. Instead of common dung, I have been soaking the hides in a bark stew. We will visit the beamhouse soon enough for you to see the process first hand."

The sun continued its slow descent. A translucent lavender curtain covered the verdant fields. Parting the grass, a cougar head peered. A flaxen-haired girl wrapped in a green speckled pelt pounced forward. Her piercing, azure eyes scanned the

Qual visitors as if prey. Four domesticated cats followed as she meowed with clenched hands. The girl's forearms were colored as if she had been splashing in molten emerald. Helen's eyes locked with Sharon's, then widened as she saw Lacey. The doll's glass eyes looked too real. Could they see things humans could not? What have those glass orbs observed? As Helen mused, she was oblivious to the presence of adults.

"You dyed Helen's pelt?" Lord Don asked.

"Me? No." Helen's father chuckled. "She thought the cauldron of dye contained fairy light. She wanted Angie colored the same. At least I stopped her before she took a full bath in it."

Lady Nadeen's frown showed her welling disapproval. She pulled Sharon tighter against her hip.

Helen prowled up beside them, peering around Nadeen's dress, pressing her hands against the fine cloth. Nadeen rotated to protect her daughter and her own finery, caught in the middle of childish play. The more she turned, the more Helen giggled. Sharon began laughing too, thinking it safer for her mother to step away.

"Now Helena," the burly furrier spoke his daughter's formal name so she knew he was serious, "do not touch our guest's dress with those dirty paws."

Don added, "You two should go play." Nadeen's eyes shot to him. It was improper to argue with her husband, even in this setting. Her thoughts roared: *'If anything happens to her... Don? Don, why are you not looking at me? Really? She is only eight years old. Are you going to let her run out there without adult supervision?'*

Smiling, Helen took Sharon's hand. She led her friend away.

"Have fun!" The wigged regent placed a calming hand on his wife's shoulder as the girls departed. Lady Nadeen sighed, biting back her concerns and bottling her temper.

For a few minutes, the parents talked outside. New methods of textile making could rejuvenate the devastated clan. They had to continue developing their craft. What else could they do but proceed as if the past nightmares were not going to return? The sorcery of the gods could not be controlled or predicted. The parents lost sight of Helen and Sharon, so they moved inside to continue their conversation.

Hand-in-hand, the girls giggled while crossing the meadow. Four cats followed on their heels. Helen led her friend to a clearing beneath a mature briar patch. The setting sun streamed through the network of thorny stems that arched over their heads. Helen plopped down upon the ground and lay upon her back. Snowy strutted over, stepped atop her chest, and then continued back into the thatch.

Sharon caught her breath while remaining standing. Spotty rubbed cheeks against her cordage basket. "What is she doing?"

"He must like how you smell."

"I smell? But I wash every day." Sharon sniffed her dress.

Helen giggled. "Like lye and lavender."

"My Mum's perfumed soap! I smell like my mother?" Sharon was more proud than aghast at the revelation. "She says lavender keeps insects away. She also says I shouldn't sit in dirt."

Shadow deposited a dead mouse beside Helen. The offering fell atop a collection of disembodied teeth and claws. Helen had saved all the trophies the cats had brought her. She was a curious explorer who empathized with the larger animals her dad skinned; she stole away many abject relics from his tanning workshop.

Helen noticed Sharon playing with a rocking tooth. "I have lost seven now. Can I have that?"

Sharon flushed with embarrassment. "It'll bleed if it comes out! Mum will be mad if I dirty my dress. Young ladies shan't get dirty, she says." Worried about such transgressions, she stepped onto a rock to distance herself from the loamy soil.

"It's too dry to worry about. See?" Helen showed her hands. The nails were stained lime-green, and her forearms spotted, likewise. She rubbed her hands together and some dust flew, yet no dirt stuck. It had not rained for days and the ground was solid. Helen watched Sharon check her loose tooth again. "Come on, can I pull that out?"

"Not ready yet." Sharon reluctantly pulled up her skirt and knelt on her bare legs, "Let's play city-like. We can have a dinner party." Sharon placed Lacey on the ground in a sitting position. Sharon unlatched the tasseled button on her basket. Helen moved close expecting sparkling treasure. Sharon removed a translucent, forest-glass pitcher and four ceramic teacups adorned with floral patterns; one cup had cracked during transit.

"That one is gorgeous!" Helen extended her hands to take it.

"It's cracked, careful!" Sharon's frown turned to a smile as she observed Helen cradle the damaged teacup. Helen always saw something special in things that other folk deemed spent. She loved that about her friend.

Helen stared at the cracks as if scrying some fortune. "What does your Mum say about taking such nice cups to play with?"

"My Papa let me have these. He doesn't want them back. I wished that one hadn't broken though."

"It's not broken." Helen poured fictitious tea from the jar into it and pretend to drink. "It works fine."

Queen-Bee strode up to the cups and sat down as if an honored guest. She was regal in pose. Her eyes squinted closed as she rotated her head toward each as if expecting a bow. She ignored a firefly hovering past to land on Lacey's right glass eye. Sharon shooed it away, then stuffed Lacey in the basket for protection.

"Please don't hide her." Helen said. "You must let Lacey drink tea with us. She is one of us."

"Yes, of course. I was just going to move her closer to me. Lacey needs watching over, else she runs off," Sharon explained bringing the doll out again. "Everyone in Qual gets a doll when they are young. My Papa made mine with lace from his ancestors, but he got the leather from your Da. We should get you a doll."

"I'll be fine with Angie. She watches over me real well,"

Helen stroked her pelt. Feeling the need to move, she rose. "Do city folk dance at dinner parties?"

"Yes!" Sharon's eyes sparkled. She clapped her hands. "Let's have a cotillion now. I've seen them in Qual's manse. Up, now. Curtesy. Now, grab a partner." Helen removed Angie from her shoulders and held each forepaw in her hand. Sharon held Lacey likewise. "Now let us form a square." They held hands and twirled. They then reversed, twirled faster, and again, until both grew so dizzy that they spun to the ground. Then Smokey and Shadow jumped on them, joining in the fun.

The twilight was darkening. Insects appeared in larger numbers. Regaining composure, the girls sat upright. Helen called the next task, "We must be getting to the fireflies."

"You mean lightning bugs?" Sharon panted still. "They hold lightning for sure. Their glow is blueish."

Helen countered. "To me they look yellow-green, as if their bodies held a sun inside. I think they feed off it. No matter. Whatever color they are, or whatever we call 'em, they are our children. Quick! We'll collect them, save from the harms of the wild. They do not know the danger they are in! Silly children."

Lacey, via Sharon's puppeteering, paraphrased her Mum's advice. "My children have escaped again and run in the fields. We must protect them from the wasps!" Sharon rose holding the green pitcher. Emboldened with Lacey and Angie, the girls darted after the glowing bugs. Helen caught one in a two-handed grab. She brought the specimen unharmed to the motherly doll. Lacey scolded it for leaving her side, only to praise it immediately after for being a lovely child. It was then dumped into the decanter. Sharon's hand served as a lid.

"Angie will rescue the little ones!" The pelt's appendages spread, assuming the shape of angel wings. Helen swooshed ahead. Four cats followed. In minutes, flashing lights filled the jar.

The girls caught a few dozen before reconvening under the domed briar patch. Sharon overturned the glass to contain the flashing flies. Helen plucked brambles off her pelt, then she adjusted the city girl's bonnet.

"Is it not centered properly? I had tied it tightly."

"Too centered, actually." Helen loosened a strap and skewed it. "It shouldn't be that perfect after such an adventure. You must look the part." She paused, sniffing suddenly. "Do you smell that?"

Sharon inhaled the dusk air. Smoke rich with roasted meat and caramelized apples reached them. "Is that dinner? Quick, another round of tea before they call us in." Sharon filled the cups with air. Spotty investigated the empty teacup in Sharon's hands with bewilderment, then the cat rocked it by marking it with her forehead. As before, Queen-Bee stationed herself equidistant between the girls.

Helen shared her invisible tea with Angie, and then drank a full swill herself. "All this tea makes my bladder full. I think I shall make water soon."

"Out here in the fields?"

"What would your Mum say about that?"

Sharon snorted a laugh. "In the city, we'd do that in a pot."

"A teapot? Gross."

"No," Sharon giggled, "into a *chamber* pot. Collectors trade coin for such water. Then they sell it to master craftsman, apothecaries and such." The fireflies ceased buzzing about. "Oh, look, our children grow tired. Can they breathe in there?"

"Time to release them." Helen agreed. "Make a wish for what you want to become when you grow old. Now, place your hands on the jar with mine."

Together, lifting the jar, they exclaimed: "one... two... three... you are free!"

Sharon asked, "What did you wish for?"

Helen was still gazing at the departing fireflies. "To see like a fairy. You?"

"To serve a lord craftsman."

"Do you mean marry?" Helen's eyes widened and mouth opened astonished.

Sharon giggled and blushed. "Marry? No. Lords also have servants and courtiers. Not just wives."

"Does your Papa have servants?"

"Well, he once did. They disappeared." She shook her head to dispel the memories. "Even with abductions, the city still has people. Although the manor house is rather empty now. I play inside mostly. Outside can be dangerous. Mum says it is best to play inside where the birds and wasps cannot get you. Sometimes Cecelia visits when her mother comes."

Helen twirled her hair contemplating being inside so much. She grimaced.

"We expect to move into Qual's mansion soon. You

would adore the tapestries in the Hall of Mirrors."

"I imagine Qual as a maze of walls. No grass or trees."

"Hmmm, we have some trees. Believe me, it can be fun." Sharon said. "You want to visit? You must feel lonely out here by yourself."

Helen considered her cats and friend Angie. "I don't feel lonely."

"You shall visit me, regardless. So I will be less alone."

Helen grasped Sharon's hands. "It is settled then. We'll ask my Da tonight."

The sky darkened precipitously. Distant shouts from their parents became muffled under sudden, roaring winds.

"They call for us. Must be time for a real dinner."

Playtime was at an end. In less than an hour's span, the two enjoyed a lifetime of scenarios. They danced, chased bugs, had a tea party, and dreamt of their future. They stood to return, but strong gusts knocked the girls to the ground.

Helen and Sharon struggled to open their eyes. They saw wraiths swimming in the sky and effigies of mantises, and they heard the desperate screaming of their parents. Each blade of grass bent like a finger, suddenly alive. The field, now a blanket of hands, grabbed the girls and hugged them tight, the storm raging over them remained hot and furious. Angie wrapped Helen as surely as Lacey crawled atop Sharon to shield against the volcanic froth. Unable to breathe, they lost consciousness.

Dyscrasia was not eliminated from the Land, as the parents had feared. To the west, a battle raged between a skeletal warrior and an impregnated eldritch god. Her earthly womb had been sliced opened. The event shook the earth and spewed forth plumes of ash; a litter of eggs and hybrid wraiths was unleashed. The goddess and her army of enthralled pawns, including Clanlord Qualenson and his son Urlquason, were killed. Their ghosts joined the debris clouds. The sentient storm rolled over the girls…

HELEN AWOKE INSIDE a dust cloud, cat paws nudging her cheek. She pushed to a kneeling position atop a dune of ash. Shaking the warm powder from her hair and off her cougar pelt, she looked around to see who had awoken her. It could have been Smokey, or his sisters, Shadow and Spotty; or perhaps their mother, the orange-stripped Queen-Bee. Whichever one it was, it had retreated ten yards and was now veiled behind dense swirls. A colorless calamity obscured all. There was no horizon to ground her vision. Dizzy, she placed her hands down. Her head throbbed.

Right before the sky collapsed, she had heard her parents yelling. What happened?

Helen pulled her pelt around her and arose shakily. "Angie, our dreams turn sour."

Well beyond the cat, a distorted, warm glow shimmered and marked an obscure horizon. Its nimbus of tangerine and lemon hues pervaded the smoky fog. Between the girl and this fiery light, icy-blue motes wisped about frantically. They glowed like miniscule stars dropped from the heavens to become ensnared in earth's gravity. A bodiless humming reverberated in the air. The cat twisted her head to survey the lights and sounds.

"Spotty, is that you?" Helen called. The unidentified cat ignored her. It remained afar.

Something else had answered her. Beside the cat, the ground swelled. A grotesque silhouette arose. Was it a creature from the storm? Helen could hardly move despite her heart racing. She was too disoriented to run. The shadowy figure grew taller and taller from behind her pet. The cat darted into the fog as the shade approached. Then the newcomer stumbled forward, covered in gray dust.

Helen brushed ash away from her eyes. "Sharon?"

Sharon sneezed. Sooty snot pooled onto her lip. She kept her hands clasped to the elaborate leather doll. Its glass eyes and silk ribbons were as soiled as its owner. She stood awkwardly, being in shock.

The buzzing amplified suddenly, preceding a swarm of bright, cerulean things. Evil wasps hovered in an undulating cloud. These were not part of the original storm, but came now to search the burnt earth. Each scavenger was bigger than a child's hand, much larger than any natural creation. The swarm was on a collective mission. It circled for a time, then accelerated toward whatever it hunted.

Helen grabbed Sharon's hand and pulled her down. She used her pelt to cover both her and her friend. When the buzzing dissipated, they stood again. The wasps had vanished from sight. A quiet pulsing murmur confirmed that they had not gone far. "Come. Our fireflies have all gone away. The wasps have taken their place."

Sharon resisted. Did she not recognize her friend?

"It's me. *Helen*. Let's go to my home. Our mamas and papas are there. Come now, I will guide us."

Shuffling through the devestated field, Helen led Sharon. They stumbled twice on debris hidden by smooth drifts. Helen thought she knew where her cabin was, but the landscape was different now. The crest and troughs of the hills were oriented in unfamiliar ways. Vegetation was all but eliminated. Landmark trees were absent or burnt beyond recognition. The dust-saturated sky limited vision to mere yards. Their feet tangled with bundles of bent grass.

"I thought my home would be around here."

Sharon trembled. She muttered with a frown, "We are lost."

"Maybe." Helen would not succumb to fear just yet. There were always ways to get unlost, after all. However, she was far from comfortable. Helen began to chill in the eerie mist. Prickly goosebumps riddled her skin as she pondered where to go next.

In lieu of a doting mother and a city which assured shelter and wise adults, Sharon had to rely on her friend. She would have succumbed to outright panic alone in the nightmarish countryside. At least with her companion, Sharon could maintain a dumbfounded state laced with hope.

The vague sun-like orb still shone through the fog. It promised warmth if nothing else. Helen marched toward it. Persistence brought them closer and closer to the light. It took an hour to walk a quarter mile. Blue specks continuously threaded the fog. Dissonant buzzing persisted. Life as they had known it was mysterious sinking under the obscuring miasma. Each moment they failed to clarify where their parents were and what happened to the land, uncertainty grew inside their minds as a cancer. Breathing became difficult, whether it be toxic vapors or anxiety compressing their lungs. They had to break free of this low-hanging cloud. Stalks of burning nettles occasionally grabbed them like ghostly hands. So much ash had fallen that they often tripped on branches or divots; there was a cushion of dying embers beneath, which would steam when exposed.

Eventually, they crested a knoll. The warm glow was closer now. It was not the sun after all—just burning ruins. Helen's homestead. What had been a cluster of cabins for tanning and preparing fur for Clan Qual, was now a fire-pit. Demonic wasps danced in the pumpkin-hued flames.

Helen wrapped herself tight. "Angie? We need you now. Help us find our parents." A pulse of warmth ran through her. The guardian pelt had responded. Without Angie, Helen would have been utterly lost. With her, she was bolstered to carry on. Emboldened with naive confidence, Helen approached the flames. "Come, Sharon. We must find them."

"Stop!" Sharon intervened, snapping out of her shock to save her friend. "You'll burn."

Helen escaped her grip and advanced a few feet. Invisible heat forced her to stop. Sharon was right: it was too hot.

They hugged and cried. Lacey was at their center, Angie wrapping them all. Soot stained their torn clothing. Sharon's mother would have been furious.

Sharon cried, "Mum said doom would come. Qual is cursed. Even out here in the country. They are gone."

"Nonsense. Can't you hear them? They are alive."

"That's just crackling wood, Helen. Mum knew this would happen. Do not pretend anymore."

"I'm not pretending!"

Suddenly a plank shifted. Embers shot into the sky. Wasps came to investigate this disturbance.

Queen-Bee dragged Spotty's singed carcass from the wreckage, her own fur smoking. Her prodding did not revive her calico daughter. Angie's paws, via Helen, extended for Queen-Bee. The tabby ran away in grief. Helen lifted Spotty's burnt body.

"See, all will be fine," Helen hugged the carcass.

The cat was clearly dead, but Sharon was too overwhelmed to try and educate her friend. Then she heard rustling from afar. "Someone comes. Maybe it is Mum."

"Or Papa?" Helen asked, eyes wide.

Sharon pointed away. "No. It comes from the road. From Qual city." Swirls assumed effigies of avian and insectan faces in the churning fog. As the ghostly figure approached, the luminous insects near it lost their light and fell dead. "I see three people!"

"Uh, Sharon. That's one... body... but it has multiple heads. Hide!"

Both simultaneously dropped to their bellies. They watched in curiosity. The horror they observed was complex.

Monstrous faces coalesced in the roiling vapors, yet it was a single wraith that shuffled forth on three human legs; a huge fourth hind leg was crippled, shaped like that of a cricket's, and functioned only partially. It had three heads: a hairless human head lay limp on its right shoulder—its torso and legs merged with that of a giant bird; flanking the left, a tusked ant-head drooped lifeless; only the middle avian head appeared cognizant. A mixture of articulated long arms and shorter agile ones sprouted from the central abdomen. Many awkwardly-bent limbs shook with palsy. Three sets of wings emerged from a mass of exposed entrails, but it appeared too crippled to fly. Dozens of mutant appendages sprouted from the trailing posterior, all connected with glossy tissue, which wriggled like legs of a millipede.

The thing went directly to the cabin. Vapors from the wraith's body were incompatible with the energy within the wasps. Its presence immediately quenched the life out of them. The monster was not concerned about the heat or flames either, even though its skin blistered. Its lengthy beak combed the coals. The mutant dug through the embers frantically, and emerged with arms full with four smoking bodies. Loaded, it hastily headed back where it came from.

"They… are… dead." Sharon muttered. She sat up, lightheaded.

"Sharon, your Mum's eyes were open. My Da's too. They are alive! I saw 'em." Helen said caressing her dead cat. She motioned to give chase. "We can't let it take our parents. Let's go after it."

Sharon sat crying. "A… demon… took them…"

Helen grabbed her friend's wrist, but Sharon broke away.

"Come on." Helen squatted behind Sharon, wrapped her arms about her friend's waist, and lifted. Once standing, they faced. Their eyes met in a confused duel. One set reddened with grief, tears flowing over swollen cheeks; the other, wide-eyed with madness. "It's leaving. Let's follow. Can you walk?"

Sharon stumbled, then sat in defeat.

Helen had observed this behavior before. Her cats acted funny like this. Sometimes they became melodramatic. Giving them attention would drive them to turn their noses and go a few steps away.

Helen surveyed the gray horizon and announced, "We can't let it go out of sight. It doesn't move very fast. I've seen snails go faster. Still, we are going to lose track if we don't get going." Her friend did not move. "Fine, I'll go ahead. You stay here. I can come back once I know where it's going."

"Don't leave." Sharon said suddenly.

Helen turned and feigned going away. They were not divided for more than a moment. Despite grieving, Sharon had not the heart to stay by herself. Of course, Helen did not have the conviction to abandon her.

Sharon trailed behind her playmate. They staggered northwest behind the crippled monster. It was tough to discern details. Shadows shrouded the bodies. Smoke emitted from them, obscuring the view. Sharon's heart raced. Her Papa's head bobbed below his waist, his wig hanging like a huge half-peeled scab. Her Mum was bent over a shoulder facing away—her legs secured by a grotesque, elbow-less arm. Perhaps under all that burnt skin, they were still alive! Or, was her friend just seeing things again? She had to keep up regardless. They ran atop the ground that used to be the road to Qual. All the beautiful lightning bugs were gone now, replaced with wasps. Only the atmosphere surrounding the wraith was free of the poisonous blue insects. The verdant hills were all covered in heaps of charnel powder. Everything was smoothed or flattened.

Eventually, the conjoined monster led them to a strange terrain. Here polished, egg-shaped boulders dotted the area. Many rested within craters. Several were cracked and leaked white, amniotic jelly. Here and there, appendage-less forms encrusted with eyeballs and ears sat motionless, their orifices likewise dripping pearly ichor. Although bizarre, these vestiges of life appeared too malformed to be a threat.

The girls sought refuge behind the stone shells. Helen asked, "Were these rocks always on the road to Qual?"

Sharon shook her head in the negative.

"Did they drop from sky during the storm? Or were they expelled from earth?" Helen wondered.

"They look like eggs," Sharon whispered.

The girls concealed themselves behind an oval boulder while peering at the alien mutant.

Surrounded by its dead siblings, the bird-man-insect hobbled toward an enormous wall woven with human bodies, ragdolls, and willow branches. Hordes of cerulean wasps infesting the barrier suddenly died mid-air as the wraith approached.

Those near it became discolored then sank to the earth, poisoned by the creature's presence. Many wasps sought refuge within the piled bodies, burrowing into flesh. The wraith paid no heed to the bugs. It laid the girls' parents on the pile then worked them into the fabric of the wall.

Helen had witnessed birds and ants behave similarly in the wild. "It's making a nest."

The wraith bent its head downward and plucked its tumorous abdomen. It pulled at its own flesh, causing it to bleed. White ichor spurted like milk from a mother's breast. It sprayed the embryos within the nest.

"What is it doing?" asked Sharon.

Helen responded, "I think it is nursing. But the babies seem dead."

"Gross."

The wraith glanced toward them.

"Duck!" Sharon pulled Helen down to cower with her. Compelled to know what the wraith was doing, Helen peered around the shell. The wraith continued fixing the nest, then departed northwest doubtlessly to collect more material.

"Quick, while it's away. We have to save 'em."

Helen still clung to her dead cat as she ran to her father. From the knotted cruor, her father's torso hugged his daughter. He bled on her. Wasps began surfacing from within his meaty biceps. Anxious to free him, she pulled on his arm. "You are stuck, Da."

"Helen," her father rasped. His furs melded with his scorched skin so he looked like a burnt bear. He attempted to adjust the pelt with his exposed hand. "Angie will be taking care of you."

Helen tugged again. His skin peeled off as if a glove. "We need help, Sharon. A doctor too."

Sharon cried, embraced Lacey, and shielded her eyes. Did her friend not know her father was dead? That their parents were anchored into the nest, and even if freed would be too heavy to carry? How could Helen not sense reality? Their parents were gone. Now her friend was talking to her Mum whose left shoulder protruded from the rotten dam. But Mum's lips did not move! Either a ghost was talking to Helen, or her friend was going insane. Helen imagined things too well before the storm. Who knew what was real anymore? Sharon's tears wetted Lacey.

"Now Sharon, your Mum says that ladies don't cry in public."

Sharon gasped. Crawlers were on her wrists and scuttling on Lacey. She could hardly believe her eyes. So close, she saw that these wasps were not normal. They had human faces, and arms! Mum always said: 'beware the bugs.' Called them demons. Sharon brushed several off her doll, but they just flew in a circle to return. A score of these glowing man-bugs dug into Lacey's stuffing. She shook the doll to dislodge most. Then she twirled in a circle, with Lacey in her outstretched hands, so that spinning forces would eject the invaders.

"Sharon, this is no time for dancing," Helen said with her right hand on a hip, her left hand cradling Spotty. The insectan minions emerged faster and faster from the corpses.

Keening wasps came out from the bodies. They clustered about Lacey and Spotty.

Sharon stared at the wasps on her doll and friend's cat in horror. They were brighter and bluer than lightning bugs, more than any moonlight. They began to dig into the toy and carcass. What did they want? Suddenly, the visible wasps dulled and literally turned into stone. Sharon alerted, "It's coming back!"

"We can't go yet."

"Helen, come on. It will see us."

"We haven't freed 'em yet!"

A ghastly silhouette lumbered forward, entering the nest a hundred yards away from the girls. The wraith approached, holding a bundle of fresh prey. It had returned with variegated artifacts clutched against its cyst-ridden chest. The more it shuffled, the more it extracted the color from its myriad dolls, stray banners, and dyed fabric. Step by step, the objects became duller and duller. All turned gray. Consuming the color, its primary spine became increasingly erect.

The wraith padded the nest with spent ornaments. It sensed the young infiltrators again. The beaked head pivoted skyward, then it rotated so its ears listened across the area. Homing in on the children, it lowered its head at them. It advanced spasmodically, squawking, and chomping its mandibles. Its cricket leg stretched forward, then bent, then extended again. Opposite, one wing unfurled, lowering its talons to claw the ground, pulling it forward. Dead limbs collided with animated appendages as it struggled to move: the human side trembled vigorously; sparkling spittle exuded from its rotting human mouth; its insectan tusks clanked with alternating strides.

Desperate to save her Da, Helen remained. She tugged harder and harder on him, to no avail.

He spoke, "Helen, calm now. It's all a dream. Sweet darling, it's just playtime."

"Da, you are not good at acting."

"True. Children always fantasize better than us old folk. Your Ma is even worse than me. Don't let playtime get the better of you though. You little ladies will find a way out."

"Da. Don't fade. I need you."

"Fear not. Your guardian Angie is with you. Go!"

Then the woven boughs swallowed him. Helen stepped away, walking slowly backward from the nest and the encroaching wraith. Putrid rank preceded the creature. Wasps failing to reach shelter fast enough dropped as petrified shells. From the mutant's abdomen, three hands groped with broken fingers.

Helen growled, empowered by Angie. Crouching, one hand clutched flaccid Spotty while the other prepared to claw.

Sharon watched in horror. Helen's hair lost what little color it had, becoming bleached white. The green splotches in her friend's hands faded to gray. Sharon jerked Helen away. "Even if you were a lion you couldn't fight that. Now, come on!"

Helen hissed.

Sharon grabbed the scruff of Helen's neck, her hand clamping onto Angie. Sharon leaned away, removing Helen. "Snap out of it!"

The looming wraith advanced faster.

They had to withdraw, or else be eaten.

Sharon kept tugging until Helen locked eyes with hers in annoyance. They stared deeply for a crucial moment, just long enough for Helen to consider reason. She had to relent her desire to play with her father. Transforming into a ferocious cat would not protect her. It was time to go.

"Run!" They shouted together.

The girls amassed momentum. Ashen whirlwinds rose from their footsteps. Both sprinted clutching a broken form, be it cat or leather doll. They retreated wildly, ignorant of any remaining corruption in the things they carried.

The wraith gave chase. Shuffling irregularly, its upper portions swayed. The rhythmic clacking of tusks receded while they escaped. As terrifying as it was in appearance, it lacked any speed. Burdened with the weight and awkwardness of dead limbs, the conjoined wraith could not catch the girls.

Eventually, the two felt they had evaded the beast. However, they were utterly lost. Exhausted, breathless, and out of their minds, they collapsed somewhere in the countryside. Sleep took them swiftly. The girls lay vulnerable, unaware of the lingering wasps secreted within Lacey and Spotty.

II: Puppets' Theater

"**W**HY DID YOU *spare me, apostate?*" Doctor Grave asked telepathically while hiding from his new master.

Lord Endenken Lysis considered a response. From atop the mountainous Chromlechon, the skeletal warrior stared toward the distant horizon. Constellations dazzled his undead vision. These distressed him. Every spark of light could have been a star, a sun, or god's fire—had he been staring skyward. As it was, he stared downward at the Land's surface. The motes were not celestial lights. They were the desperate souls of the living, roaming the wild night for a respite from immeasurable pain. Lord Lysis returned, *"I inherited hell. You will aid me in repairing humanity."*

"But you prevailed! It is my eldritch kin who are in need of repair. My queen...," Doctor Grave mindspoke.

"I need you up here, not reading my mind from afar. Where are you cowering, Grave?"

The golem doctor ignored his new master, and continued

with his rant. *"Deceiver, why did you violate your family's legacy? Their faith? Their muse?"*

Lysis withdrew from the peak, and strode past soot-laden corpses. Petrified bodies, both anthropoidal and hybrid, littered the grounds. Scavenger birds fed on the carnage near the colony's surface—the meat being mostly human. Gaping cave entrances pockmarked the porous mountain. He descended. In place of vultures, rats busied themselves in the darkness. The lower he went, the more numerous were the carcasses of elder insects and mutant harpies. Tangled heaps of battling warriors stood frozen in frenzied stances, turned to stone via alchemy. Gnarled appendages reached upwards like trunks of vegetation.

Lysis glared into the Doctor's ruined Dissection Theater. It was here that Endenken Lysis and the Doctor had initiated their last battle. The skeleton of an avian god had once reinforced the Theater's vaulted ceiling, but this was swallowed by the floor when Lysis used his magical sword, *Ferrus Eviscamir*, to carve the earth. Now colossal, skeletal wings extended through the toppled strata, serving as disjointed support structures or rungs for climbing to lower levels. In many ways, it appeared as if the skeleton did not belong to the original god, but to the earth instead. Indeed, if the bones had flesh now, it was soil, clay, and stone.

The Theater seemed abandoned, save for a young boy on stage. He appeared colorless, but a silvery nimbus sparkled about him—or perhaps *from inside* him. Cracks in his skin glowed bright, as if a sun burned from his heart. Limned sloughs of his skin became increasingly translucent. Cradled in his arms was a desiccated, avian embryo as large as a wild turkey. Blazing, white-hot tears streaked from the ill child's eyes. This ichor soaked into the dry flesh of the motionless form he hugged.

Eucrasiac blood also seeped from seams in the boy's limbs, from segments where elbows bent and appendages joined to his torso. The fowl-like wraith gained energy from the liquid offering. Soon the deceased, winged form sprang to life. The avian puppet's eyes adopted the brilliance of its childish master: colorless yet intense. It wriggled free of the child's grip. The fowl hopped about until it joined two other magically-animated, rag dolls that stood near the primary operating table. Both dolls' eyes blazed. One, depicting an injured, princely warrior, was missing an arm. The other was its royal mother, an eidolon of a lady from Clan Tonn, impaled with an iron needle.

An audience of a dozen human children sat observing the performance. They loved to watch Echo entertain. The Gray Foundling was not wholly human, however, the children were not afraid of his enlarged, lidless eyes or reflective skin. Nor did his narrow, pointed jaws, which resembled insectan mandibles, cause alarm. They saw him as a moderator between the old, dead world and the new, strange one. His similar age and desire to play helped this.

The gray boy began his performance by controlling the one-armed puppet. "For Aleece!" Echo repeated the warrior's battle cry. The maimed knight engaged the prancing fowl-wraith, ever approaching his goal: the impaled lady. Echo swayed his lengthy arms, orchestrating the dolls' actions. They moved synchronously with him, being possessed by his ichor. The fowl struck out with its lengthy beak. The warrior doll and his lady held their ground, but they were not supposed to stay standing. That was not how the Ill Age played out. To play according to history, Echo's hand swooped down. The impaled doll was knocked off the table, into a black puddle. The wraith-fowl followed waving ripped wings.

The audience gasped, then four girls and three boys rushed toward the stage to gaze into the puddle, to get a closer look. They did not get there.

They were not as fast as the bossy, royal from Qual who managed to intercept their path. She was in the right to protect them, since the area around the stage was dangerous, marked with holes and bottomless pits. The freckled, orange-haired babysitter, a child herself, was concerned about rules and ensuring safety—values she learned from Qualenson Manor. Her pigtails, strung with beaded glass that glistened like rubies, matched her stockings: knee-length hosiery, striped in bands of yellow and pink. Her wardrobe consisted only of a dull linen shift. Pale skin amplified the reds in her socks and hair. Her heels touched, her back was straight, but her arms were in constant motion. They moved from resting on her hips, to crossing her chest, to pointing and nudging the others back into safer positions. Soon they were all seated again.

"Echo, your audience becomes more transfixed as your productions become more complex." Lysis interrupted the play. His voice sent the orphans deeper into the shadows. "Have you seen the Doctor?"

"Doctor," the boy repeated, holding the one-armed warrior doll while pointing toward a pit in the floor. He then returned to reenacting the warfare ending the Ill Age.

Lysis climbed down this shaft through sundered strata to arrive in the abandoned nursery. Here the Doctor kneeled before the reanimated carcass of his ant queen with the spectral memories of his crystallized wife and daughters bearing witness. The masked golem rested his head against the cyclopean ant, the undead goddess who was in a comatose state. White blood leaked from Grave's chest about *Ferrus Eviscamir's* signature mark. He sat in a bed of broken glass. Those crystals had once been the flesh of his family.

"Your queen and family are gone. You owe your life to me."

"Am I alive?"

Lysis unsheathed his sword *Ferrus Eviscamir.* "Call me 'Lord'. And stand up."

"Aye, Lord."

"Stop speaking into my head. When we are close, talk aloud."

Grave mumbled an assent, and then spoke, "Lord, why sustain me? You need not waste your power."

"I only keep you from a true death because I need access to your arcane knowledge."

"Yet you possess my queen too," Doctor Grave said while stroking the carcass of the eldritch ant. "Can she not aid you? She created me, and was the ultimate source of power for your Pictish ancestors."

"Had her psyche survived, I would not need you. She is no longer of sound mind, so I animate her insectan body as a steed. You no longer serve her, and she no longer rules. She is a once-Queen. Call her such."

The doctor's hood of flayed skin hid his disdain, but his aura spoke true and openly to Lysis's undead sight. Grave's mind delved into the queen's memories, ruminating on his service, then reflecting on the last of her brood. Then the golem thought of his own family: his elemental wife Fae and daughters. He had failed them. The Doctor pressed a hand against his aching heart. He flicked a bit of white blood weeping from his chest and licked it. It tasted like stone. Cold, molten rock.

"That is my blood, Doctor. I have conquered the dyscrasiac elders and freed you. Now you need to cooperate."

"You conquered my patronage as well as the elders' life," Grave countered. "You may own the ichor animating me, but my motivations remain tied to my memories, my history… the same Pictish muse your ancestors worshipped."

"Enough!" Lysis extended his hand and clenched it. In response, ethereal veins tightened on the golem's homunculus heart. This slowed the blood flow. Crystals formed, like needles of hoarfrost, inside arteries. Grave became paralyzed. "Doctor, your allegiance and my family's faith consumed the people across the Land. You have a new mission, serving the surviving children."

Tendrils of energy threaded between the queen and golem. Obligations and memories tied Grave to the eldritch ant. These were not two-way ties. The queen did not share Grave's emotions. Her colony and her ambitions were dead. Her body was riddled with larvalwyrmen and Lysis' ichor. She was possessed completely. Her servant not so. The golem would not turn on his own accord.

Lysis saw Grave attempt to cast some spell, to inspire the queen to action!

"Obey me!" *Ferrus Eviscamir* lashed out, cutting the astral connections.

"Be warry," Grave wheezed in aguish. Frozen and unable to retreat, he knew what was to come. "Cut away too much, and I may be of no use to you. You will cull my knowledge. And memories…"

Then Lysis saw his wife, Maeve—Grave's daughter—take form in the ether. Lysis hesitated. Maeve's vestiges were preciously scarce, since her soul was lost with her body. "Summoning illusions won't stop me!" The Gray Lord commenced with precision to preserve some of Grave's aura. "You forged the blade well. I am its new master, as I am yours." *Ferrus Eviscamir* cut more of the ghostly network between the once-Queen and the golem. These filaments turned opaque, took tangible form, and fell as brittle shards. Shattered memories of Grave joined his wife Fae's remains.

"You are indeed adept at using the sword's magic," said Grave. "My mind now clears." The golem's fiery soul settled and his demeanor changed. His innate purpose to serve was renewed. The Doctor approached his new master, hands reaching out with probing fingers. "Lord, your body needs tending."

Lysis pushed him away. "I am fine. Give me space."

Suddenly, Echo's skewered lady-puppet slid down the shaft of bones, being chased by the wraith-fowl, which was in turn pursued by the warrior doll. Echo followed, orchestrating this hunt. Several children from the Theater would be trailing to watch or seek.

"Lord, that boy has signatures of chromanti in his soul. Let me kill him."

"Leave Echo alone, Doctor. He is not a threat. Address him as a Lord too."

"The hybrid foundling? But he is dangerous by his very nature. Can you not see that?"

Lysis said, "His blood is as eucrasaic as mine. He may not be human, but he is not ill larvae for you to slay."

"He disturbs me," Grave replied, "my Lord."

As expected, Theater children clambered into the dark chamber following Echo's trail. But not all had torches, nor were they undead to see the astral plane. It was too dark for them.

"Tend to the children. Not me or Lord Echo. They need attention. Her for example…."

The girl with auburn pigtails eventually came. Where had her friends gone? She shook with frustration. She failed to control them again. Chilling loneliness shrouded her. Then fear. She found herself intimately close to the skeletal *daimon* and the doctor. She started crying.

"Her, my Lord? Her health is well. She is breathing, safe from the horrors outside this mountain."

"Doctor, she is alone. Terrified."

"Aye, my Lord. Shall I end her misery?" Grave brandished his large cleaver.

"Do not raise that weapon!" Lysis grabbed his servant's arm. "She is scared." The skeletal lord selected a humerus from the piles of bone in the chamber. Collecting ichor that seeped from the once-Queen onto one tip, he ignited a prismatic fire with a wave of his hand. He offered this brand to the child. She accepted the lit torch reluctantly, then skittered away with haste after her friends. "We need to give them hope."

Doctor Grave pointed toward his despondent queen. "Is there any hope for her?"

"Without a doubt." Lysis climbed atop the conquered ant queen, his legs straddling her grand thorax. He called to the blood and larvalwyrmen within her carcass commanding her to rise. "Doctor, follow me to the surface. Now."

Grave scampered behind his lord dutifully. He managed to keep pace with the once-Queen's gait. They reached the top of the mountain. There, night welcomed them.

Lord Lysis surveyed the valley again. Moonlight scarcely illuminated a smoldering caldera to the North: Cypria's Gallwomb. To its east lay abandoned districts blanketed with gray ash. Closest was Clan Qual, home of the doll-makers and weavers. Beyond, was Clan Tonn, where metal smiths and stonemasons hailed. There was no torchlight or brazen fires to indicate life amongst any towns or cities.

"We need to protect the survivors," Lord Lysis declared.

"Protect whom, Lord?" The masked golem asked beside him. He too looked below with his undead vision. Sparkling embers drifted over black bogs, the marshes dense with corpses. "The Ill Age has left the world in ruin. You preside over desolation."

Lysis adjusted, glaring at Grave. The radiant, white ichor that empowered him boiled within his warped bones. "I conquered your queen's eldritch sorcery. Indeed, she is my servant as are you."

"Yes, Lord Lysis, I serve you now as I had the *once-Queen*."

"It is good for you to remember that. As I have reanimated your bodies, bringing life to the dead, I too shall revive the Land."

"True Lord, your blood animates us. But the queen's colony…."

"The Chromlechon is no longer *your* queen's domain. She is just a steed now." Lysis locked eyes with the Doctor. "This mountain, my Keep, shall be a refuge for survivors. Your machinations slaughtered nearly all the mothers and fathers in this realm. Many children remain alive. I will collect them."

"Lord, the younglings will be scared of you. Your skull-face is repulsive. They will hide. You may empathize with the humans, but you are no longer one of them. In your endeavors to vanquish your clan's religion, you have assumed the appearance of a demon." Grave continued, "You could beguile them with illusion. Manipulate their vision so that you appear living again."

"Even with such enchantments, I cannot gather them all before weather or hunger takes them."

"Lord, your dyscrasiac enemies persist as well."

Lysis affronted the doctor by advancing the ant mount. He unsheathed *Ferrus Eviscamir,* ready to strike. "Under whose colony and power do they serve, if not the once-Queen's?"

Grave cowered before the sword and the tusks of his former master. "Lord, they are independent things. As diseased mutants, the blue-bloods cannot mate. Others roam without masters. Some white-ichor wraiths persevere since you freed them from Cypria's Gallwomb. They may harm the children."

Lysis's aura sparked in frustration. "There are too many. Too spread out. Too scared."

"We could attract the children...," the Doctor began.

"Silence," Lysis dismounted, "I am thinking." He paced while Grave waited. "We must bring the orphans *to* us."

"Aye, Lord."

Lysis pointed to a spot. "We could build a bonfire. Right here, atop the mountain. I can cast a spell upon its light." He ordered Grave to exit the Keep to retrieve firewood. The once-Queen hauled large rocks to the courtyard's center. Lysis used his magical sword to carve the irregular stones into a perimeter of hewn bricks. The great pit was ready by the time Grave lumbered back. He deposited the fuel. Lysis ignited the fire.

Standing a sword's length away from his Lord, Doctor Grave spoke, "Your sorcery is required to enhance the attraction. You must offer the blood. The ichor that you empower me and the once-Queen will fuel the fire and spread your influence."

"You go beyond alchemy and geomancy in these experiments."

"I extend your power, not mine. But yes, pyromancy is new. Your bloodletting into the flames should extend the reach of your *lapis elixir*. Let the children come like moths to a flame."

Lysis stepped into the Pyre, unaffected by the heat. He sliced his left arm with *Eviscamir* and ichor seeped out. The flames sputtered, lapping the blood, then turning wondrous sky-blue and lime-green. The beacon shone into the heavens as a tower of rainbow light.

A WEEK TRANSPIRED. DOZENS of children had wandered to the Keep. The Doctor organized living quarters within the mountain. Grave went to report progress. He found his master walking amongst the urchins clustered about the Pyre. The fire's warmth did little to allay their sadness.

"Civilization begins anew," the Doctor muttered. Lysis did not turn to acknowledge him. Grave continued, "Lord, the Pyre worked. Why do you brood?"

"Our efforts are not sufficient. Hundreds more remain out there. I have ridden the countryside myself. My presence scared many away. Those I could approach were often not savable. Many had died from hunger or attack. I slew one gargoyle whilst he ate from a boy. They cannot protect themselves in the wild. This Pyre is not enough."

Grave saw into the ethereal realm and observed the ghosts of the Lord's eleven children. Lysis's inability to save his family would forever motivate him. The Doctor looked toward the horizon and took inspiration from a flock of skylarks that folded upon itself, wrapping the wind's current. "Lord, let us broaden the signal's reach. We shall make many miniature fires, give them life through sorcery to retrieve others."

"What exactly are you proposing, Doctor?"

"Give these orphans a purpose. They need to focus their mind away from their nightmares. We can have them work—"

"*You* will not enslave them!"

Grave drew back, "Lord, you misunderstand. Enlisting the aid of the children is a kindness. They can make art which can feed your power. The creative process will heal them too."

"Demonstrate." *Ferrus Eviscamir* hovered near Grave's back.

"Lord, your ichor animates me, yet your trust in me seems measured."

"My mercy extends as far as your intellect is worth, Doctor Grave. My trust extends as far as *Eviscamir's* blade."

The Doctor flinched. "Yes, of course. Then I will proceed cautiously." Grave procured some colored chalk and vellum, then beckoned a red-headed girl to the fireside. She clung to the bone torch given to her by Lysis. He spoke, "Young lady, I recall you from the below the Theater. What is your name?"

She shook, too afraid to talk. Grave offered her the chalk. She did not take it. Instead, she watched the doctor as he began drawing. Soon, she joined him sketching on a separate sheet. She drew feathered wasps gorging on kittens. Doctor Grave saw the horrid visions leave her aura to stay with the art.

"Cecelia," the girl whispered. She hesitated to reveal her full family name. She was a part of what remained of Qual's upper class. Could she trust this masked doctor?

"I sense another name about you. A companion of yours. Round faced. Swollen, long arms and legs. Knotted hair. Beady eyes. Bailey? Or is it Lacey?"

Cecelia blushed. "Bailey is my doll. He's made of socks. Got left behind. Lacey is my playmate's doll. I am afraid for her. She went to see her cat-loving friend in the countryside... the same day the storm came."

"I am going to give my own fears away now, Cecelia. To the fire which hungers for such things. Will you offer one of yours too?" The masked golem took the child by hand, and the two fed their art to the flames. The fire ate Cecelia's nightmares, destroyed her wasps. Sudden strength flared within Lysis; his aura burned brighter as the Pyre responded. Cecelia also felt calmer and happier. She ignited her torch, then walked away in wonder of its variegated flames.

The Doctor said, "Lord, you sense the reaction. Whether nightmarish or hopeful, emotions empower your magic. Your sorcery feeds on creative power. But there is more. You can raise the vellum from the ash. Go ahead, Lord, bring it to life."

Lysis knelt, putting his hand into the embers to salvage Cecelia's burnt drawing. The sheet folded upon itself in his palm. A flaming wasp emerged, then collapsed. Transforming several times, the sprite finally became a winged cat. The edges of the puppet burned verdigris. It circled about awaiting instructions.

Grave spoke to it, "Seek out Cecelia's relatives or friends, any of her clan's sons or daughters. Locate any youths. Lead them here to safety." The feline sprite's wings flapped until a strong wind lifted it into the sky, toward Qual.

III: Aesthete's Harem

Helen and Sharon awoke the next day to sun-warmed cheeks. Daylight had penetrated the fog, though its beams were diffuse. Helen felt the weight of a sleeping cat on her chest, front paws curled under its body. She felt its rhythmic purr, smelled its fetid breath. Rising, she set the carcass to the side and was relieved to see her friend beside her, holding Lacey.

"We are so alone." Sharon lowered her face. "Our parents are gone."

"They can't join us during playtime. Da said so. They don't play as well as we do anyway. Don't worry. We can handle this. Sharon, you need to open your eyes. Keeping them closed won't let you pretend any better."

Sharon squinted her eyes. She did not want to pretend. The bleak western horizon looked empty of life. "Where do we go?"

"Your home in Qual?"

"No. The entire clanhold is ruined." If not desolation,

what could Helen see?

Helen responded, "Well. This spot doesn't feel like home. We'll find one elsewhere."

They roamed for several days. They were not propelled in any one direction as much as they avoided the necrophagous wasps—unaware of those hiding inside Lacey and Spotty. Both girls' tongues stilled over time. Numbness suppressed hunger. Bodies thinned. Slowly, with fatigued strides and shuffling feet, they moved every few hours.

The boundary between imagination and reality blurred. Both continuously scanned the amorphous, confining fog for threats. At any moment, they feared, insects may swarm or a wraith may emerge to snatch them.

As Helen led, Sharon saw a vaporous effigy of the nest builder morph into existence from the underbrush, reaching out toward her friend. "Watch out!" She tugged Helen close and swatted the ghost.

"What was it?" Helen asked while whirling about, instantly observing a cluster of featherless, baby birds churn into shape. The malleable, haunted mists snapped at Sharon's red hair as if they were worms to eat.

"They'll bite you!" Helen yelled, slapping the mist. The things dissipated when touched.

Fearing contamination, they brushed themselves off, as if evil was as tangible as dust. Swirling the fog kept the scary creatures from forming. Helen took to whirling a thin branch to disturb the vapors. The girls became increasingly familiar with seeing haunts, yet they remained ignorant of their sources or motivations. They knew only that their parents had warned them about dyscrasia, and now their parents were taken by manifestations of the disease.

Night encroached. Away from familiar territory, Sharon lay sleeping beside Helen. Unable to close her eyes, Helen stared into the pall. She saw a fairy fly overhead. Helen blinked her eyes thinking it was a dream. This was nothing like the terrible wraiths. The benign phantom landed. It was a winged cat. The feline sprite's form was smaller than Spotty.

"Snowy, is that you? Queen-Bee?" No, this cat was not one of hers. This was also too small to be a real cat, plus it seemed to made from paper. All edges kindled brightly with a yellowish, emerald glow. It strode with a swagger.

"Are you a fairy?" Helen asked.

The sprite approached. It stopped out of reach, sitting and licking its paws. Its diffuse spirit surrounded the girls. Helen's coldness left her. Warmth flooded into her. She woke Sharon who rose, bewildered.

"Perhaps you are an angel?" Helen asked.

A terrible buzzing suddenly encroached. Dozens of wasps had spotted the fairy and had come to investigate it. The blue insects dived forward, but the wasps dropped like pebbles as they hit the green aura before getting close enough to sting or bite.

"Sharon, let's go!" Helen warned, "Beware, cat! Evil comes."

The sprite was nonplussed and continued to preen. Petrified wasps lay about it. Its magic had reacted with the insects. As hastily as the threat came, it diminished. Wasps also had died near the wraith with the nest. Could this *daimon* be related? Surely, this cat was less menacing than the conjoined creature. Helen hoped that the sprite had come to protect them.

The cat rose, arching its back. Then it inspected the dead bugs. After examining them, it confidently walked to Helen. Helen could swear she felt whiskers brush against her. It had marked them somehow. Now its energy swelled as it commingled with the girls' auras. Then the cat walked to the south.

"Angie's friend ventures onward." Helen grabbed Sharon. It was clear what they must do. They would follow the beautiful cat.

Eventually, it led them out of the gloom.

Clear night welcomed them. However, the girls were free from one horror only to find themselves faced with overwhelming uncertainty. No civilization was nearby. Muted by the potential consequences, they walked in silence.

T HE PAPER-CAT NEVER slowed pace. Having hiked all night long, the girls could hardly walk anymore. Each step amplified the pain in their blistered feet. Helen gathered her breath, "Well, our guide races on."

"I can hardly go further," Sharon panted. She leaned forward hugging Lacey tighter.

They slowly crested a hill. Towering in the southwest, miles away in the direction they walked, peaked the mountainous

Chromlechon. A valley of sprawling, rolling hills lay between.

"The fairy led us onto the Gorgepath!" Sharon exclaimed. Sparse pear trees and fields marked the trade route which served as an artery connecting all clans: Tonn City capped the northeastern end and the Lysis Clan's Gravenstyne Fortress capped the southwestern; Clan Qual resided at its midpoint.

Hope of finding survivors renewed their pace.

"Look!" Helen pointed to a two-story manse. Broken windows lined the first floor and a balconied turret. The silhouette appeared mostly intact, even if it was unkempt. "I've never seen such a big house."

"Well it is a mansion, but it is much smaller than Qualenson's."

The front porch had collapsed. Rotten wood sprouted mold and fungus in geometric patterns. The slimy ruins were climbable. The girls ascended the steps after the cat. The sprite's spirit illuminated the interior entrance before them, casting stark shadows from cloth-covered statues onto tiled floor. The house smelled of oiled wood. Two staircases led up into darkness.

Helen and Sharon entered, attempting to navigate the marble plinths. There must have been a dozen disproportionate sculptures in the foyer. The wide-bellied figures obstructed the view of their companion. It was easiest to track the miniature cat on their hands and knees. They scampered atop a wool rug. The sprite strutted into a chamber adjacent to the entry. There, writing desks lined a wall opposite a fireplace framed with an oak chimneypiece.

The sprite settled in the hearth, curling atop the cold

cinders. Gray, half-burnt logs ignited. Somehow the paper entity did not combust. It gathered energy from the flames. The girls rose and collected paper from atop the nearby writing desks and added them the fire.

Countless portraits decorated the walls. So many were hung, that there was little space between their frames. All were of beautiful women. The chimneypiece held a marble bust of the manor's master. A brass nameplate identified him: Aesthete SanGules. A plum-colored, velvet scarf mantled his neck. His face was gaunt. A thin mustache balanced on his top lip. His eyes emanated an eerie strength that made Helen look away. On second inspection, all the women he stared at had nameplates too. Each identified a wife with a number, incrementing from one to over thirty.

"Master SanGules had many wives," Sharon gasped.

"Can lords of manors have more than one?"

Sharon shook her head. "I never heard of such a marriage. But this place is outside of Qual." She caressed the upholstery of a divan that matched the bust's scarf, appreciating her clan's artisanship. "This is expensive fabric!"

"Soft too," Helen added. "It's like fur."

"Is this like your clan's Hall of Manners?" Helen asked.

"You mean 'Hall of *Mirrors*'? Not quite. This is smaller, and styled differently."

"Let's enjoy the warm fire." Sinking into the lounge, cradling Lacey and Spotty, bathed in warm light, they dozed before the flames. Their guardian spirit rested soundly with them.

SHARON WHEEZED WHILE Helen doubled over in a coughing fit. Both swatted the air to clear the smoke. Retreating into the foyer, they looked back to see the sprite urgently kicking its hind legs in the fireplace debris, stirring up dust. Having woken its companions, it dashed upstairs.

Sharon yawned. "What is it doing? Wait… do you hear a baby crying?"

"Yes, but its faint." Helen said. "With all the wives, the master must have had lots of babies."

"Well, one may have been left unattended. Quick, the fairy goes to it. Let us save it."

They darted up the right staircase, running into a vaulted, hexagonal bedchamber. A colonnade along the back wall opened to a curved balcony. Above the arches soared broken stained-glass windows, their art reduced to shards. Cold drafts shifted tattered curtains. At center was an enormous, canopied bed covered with rotten leaves. The debris did not stop Helen from jumping atop it.

"Muma!"

The shrill cry raised bumps on their necks.

"It sounded like it came from outside," Sharon said.

Helen bounded to the floor and went onto the balcony. She saw expansive hills and, well beyond, the impenetrable edge of fog. "The sun sets already. Wasn't it just night? How long did we sleep?"

Sharon arrived at her side. They listened intently. Wind cooled their skin as they leaned on the railing. They waited but heard no more cries.

"Hey look, the cat moves. Come along."

The fairy slinked its way to a discreet doorway hidden by drapes. It reared up on its hind legs and stretched its forelegs on the trim. Both paws pointed toward an iron key ring. Then it disappeared into the hallway. Helen grabbed the keys.

The hall was long, straight, and windowless. If it wasn't for the glowing cat, they would not have been able to see. Incense censors hung beneath each candle sconce; these separated each of the thirty narrow apartments lining the corridor. Numbered metallic plates labelled the cells like the portraits downstairs.

As they walked, Sharon explained, "These would be the servant quarters."

From Number Five's door opening, a pair of feminine hands extended. They were clutched together, and strangely, made from stone. How could one carve such a lifelike sculpture penetrating the door?

"Her door is locked." Helen said.

"What are you doing?"

Helen began unlocking all the doors. "Maybe the baby is in one of these rooms?"

Sharon looked into the open rooms. Portraits of SanGules hung in each. All had writing desks. Numbers One through Twelve had statues of pregnant women. Some sat cradling their bellies. Some lay balled up on the floor. None appeared happy. Several cells toward the end of the hall contained desiccated bodies of long-haired women wearing colorful, muslin gowns.

"Look, those must be chamber pots! Ooh, these ladies have ankle jewelry!"

"Helen, those are shackles."

"Why would the servants be chained?"

Sharon considered. "I think they were the women in the portraits downstairs."

"Waaa!" The wailing baby's cries pierced the air.

"It is getting louder." Sharon grabbed Helen's arm tight. "Is it up here?"

"It's not in any of these rooms," Helen whispered.

The fairy cat paced back and forth at the top of the stairs. They reached the landing and looked down the dark stairwell. Murky outlines of a crawling form moved at the base.

"Muma," the infant's cry echoed in the foyer.

It wiggled up a step. "Muma." It climbed another.

"There it is!" Sharon started for it. She held Lacey in her left hand while her right glided down the balustrade. "We must help the baby!"

Behind her, the cat followed down with Helen, its flames pushing against the darkness.

"Watch out!" Helen grabbed her friend's shoulder. They both stumbled on the stairs, just several steps away from the advancing form.

"Ouch! What are you doing?" Sharon turned.

"That's not... a baby."

Sharon giggled while staring up toward her friend, "I swear, you see things backward."

Propelled by two truncated arms, it dragged its legless abdomen, which resembled a wasp larva. A knot of willow branches integrated with umbilical cords were twined around its length. The fetal gargoyle advanced. Its baby face had swollen, vein-ridden cheeks. Opening its maw, it clamped its single fang into Lacey.

Sharon screamed.

Helen pulled back on her friend's shoulders, yet Sharon held tight to her doll.

The infantile thing sucked on Lacey. Two wings unfurled from its abdomen and vibrated.

Sharon yelled, "It won't let go!"

Lacey's body extended in the tug-of-war, yet the leather held. The girls retreated up a step. The thing followed with its tusk piercing the doll, slobber stretching between cheek and leather.

The magical paper-cat hissed. Its proximity caused the giant baby to gag. The saliva petrified, then broke into brittle strands. The connection severed. Now freed, the girls scrambled upstairs.

Squinting its cyan eyes, the baby reached out. "Muma!"

A race commenced.

The cat advanced in front, running up, through the bedchamber and beyond. Helen and Sharon retreated with it into the servant's quarters. The fairy waited for them near cell Twenty-Seven. Entering, they pushed a desk against the door.

Vibrating hum of wings and violent collisions followed them. The larva-baby was too heavy to fly far, and the narrow hall provided little space. Seconds later, the door thumped.

Helen and Sharon pressed against the furniture. The baby cried in periodic outbursts. During the lulls, they heard strange shuffling and sucking sounds.

"What is it doing?" Sharon asked.

"It is dragging something on the floor."

"No, that was a burp."

Helen's brows tilted while she listened. She pressed her ear against the door, then whispered back, "It's against the door. Gnashing on a bone."

The girls remained alert. They had to wait until it left or fell asleep—if it could sleep. Perturbed, the girls could not leave or relax.

Helen looked at the back wall. Above the cot, SanGules's defaced portrait hung. The word "Dey" scratched over his forehead. She stared at graffiti on the desk and walls. The sprite flared with energy as it rubbed against these letters, soaking in the spirit of the woman who had resided here.

"What does 'Dey' mean?" Helen inquired. "Is that a city word?"

Sharon shrugged. She nervously fiddled with her loose tooth as her tummy growled. Helen's stomach responded. Neither left their station against the desk.

"I am so tired." Sharon murmured, the spectral light from the sprite highlighting the bags under her eyes. "How long do we stay?"

Helen hugged her. Both smelled like wood smoke. "That thing is too weak to open the door. It'll have to leave sometime."

"Why won't it stop crying?"

Helen did not answer. She looked toward the idle cat for support. The sprite had curled up in a ball, its edges pulsing orange as if it breathed. If it was comforted being in this cell, then they could manage. The girls pinned all their hope on the cat's mood.

THEIR GUIDE PAWED at the desk. The girls widened their tired eyes, too weary to know if they had ever slumbered. All was silent now, but neither knew when the tantrum had ended.

"I think the cat wants us to leave." Helen stood.

"But what about that baby?" Sharon mouthed.

"It must be gone. It is quiet."

They pushed the desk aside gingerly then eased opened the door. The corridor was empty except for several beams of sunlight infused with dust motes. Tiptoeing out, they crept toward the master's bedchamber.

Both girls stopped in their tracks as they had stepped into a puddle of mucus. The winged creature lay sleeping in cell Twenty-One, mere feet away. A corpse's arm draped over it. The larva-baby had sucked the dried flesh from its bones.

"It ate that mistress!" Sharon gasped.

The larva-baby roused.

Helen prodded Sharon. "Fast, before it sees us." They ran down and out of the house. Any noise would not matter if they could put enough distance between themselves and that monstrosity.

Morning sunlight washed over them as they bounded onto the porch. The cat walked along a handrail waiting for them. In the distance, a brilliant signal fire burned atop the Chromlechon. It flared the same colors as the sprite. Their guide hopped down and headed there.

As they descended the porch, they were greeted with a curious plea: "Mum?"

Helen and Sharon turned their heads toward the sound, away from the house. It was close. Only twenty yards away. There they saw a giant infant, which was larger than either girl. It rested in a pile of tree limbs teething on a willow bough. Iridescent slime coated everything.

The girls looked at one another as comprehension set in: the larva-baby in the servant quarters had a sibling.

"Mummum!" The demon rose. Unlike its brother, the legless worm, this one could walk.

They sprinted away with the cat. Behind them, big-baby waddled closer, ever yelling for its mother. How long would it be until his brother joined the chase?

Ash covered many of the rolling hills. Some desolate swathes still smoldered. Helen and Sharon avoided these. They stumbled on and off the Gorgepath, straying into poppy fields and briar patches, trying to lose their predator. All energy was focused on following the paper sprite. That fairy had led them from the evil fog, found them shelter, warmed them before a chimney, and woke them to escape the infantile creatures. Now it ran fast. Into the fields, the cat went to the Chromlechon.

They moved faster than big-baby, but they could still hear it pursue. "Muma…"

The fields gave way to wetlands. Shallow ponds lay hidden amongst tall grasses. The vegetation of the marshes became increasingly less dense, and deeper. The magical cat was so lithe it fluttered through the bog, as a spark would soar over fire. It traveled faster than the girls did. Helen and Sharon entered the bogs without hesitation. They sloshed forward, trudging slowly, never losing sight of it.

Helen held Spotty above the water to keep her dry—as did Sharon with Lacey. Mud splattered their faces. The bog's bottom lowered continuously. Muck held their feet. All they had to do was reach the shoreline that abutted the slope. Wading out until their knees were covered, they plodded through the grasping hands of broken, naked tree limbs. Toxic fumes from decaying nature wore their throats more and more raw with each breath. Swarms of mosquitos converged on exposed skin.

Like a giant dragonfly, the winged larva-baby hovered behind. It surpassed the pace of its toddling brother. "Muummmm… mummmummmm…."

On a mounded path in the distance, the sprite waited for them. The girls risked pools of unknown depth to reach it. The brackish waters wetted their bellies. They trudged on until they heard splashing coming from ahead.

Something swam toward them. Yet the two infantile creatures from the manse were still somewhere behind them. Louder and louder, faster and faster, the third threat advanced.

Splashing concealed details from the finned grub-baby that approached.

Helen and Sharon stood paralyzed. The swimming mutant blocked their path to the cat. Where could they go? They were surrounded.

Sharon shivered weakly with clenched teeth. "Mum said, Mum said…"

Then from behind, big-baby crashed through the reeds. Facing them was the gaping mouth of the teething creature. It reached toward them…

And then the last brother arrived. Above them hovered the larva-baby. Cyan blood dripped onto the black water bedside them. Each drop glowed and floated like oil upon water. It curled its segmented tail, lowered, and latched onto Lacey with its little hands. Sharon held on with all her might.

Helen twirled about as a largemouth maw clamped around her dead cat. Grub-baby paddled desperately with six fin-hands, homing on Spotty. The grossly large, lower jaw enclosed on her forearm; a snake-like tongue coiled about. It nursed, gurgling a stifled, "Mamama."

Helen was like a cornered wild animal. Channeling Angie's spirit, she clawed at the slimy, scaled demon. Scratching would not release the sucker. Big-baby, with its strong arms, held Helen and Sharon as its brothers pulled at Lacey and Spotty. Neither girl would let go. They splashed back and forth generating foamy, black froth.

Wrestling with three babies, sinking in a mire, the two had little hope…

Whoosh! An abrupt wave crashed over them. Water washed over their heads, separating the cluster. Instead of battling the demons, the girls struggled to surface against angry currents. The waves abruptly settled. Standing again to catch their breath, oily muck sluiced down their heads. Algae scum clung to their clothes. Hastily they looked for the demons. Where were the babies? Before either could locate them...

Whoosh! Another sudden, enormous surge tossed them off their feet. Liquid filled Helen's ears and stung her eyes. Nearby, Sharon floated on her back, her arms and legs spread wide. Helen went to her. Sharon's eyes were open and her chest heaved. Leaches covered her brow. Helen got under her friend's shoulder and propped her upright.

The babies remained out of sight for the moment, but the source of the disruption in the bog emerged before them.

Sunlight washed over the towering skeletal warrior. Rays flared around its head so he glowed like a star. Crowned with horns, he trudged forth with a crystal sword. Each swipe of his blade cut through bog water, shooting out walls of looming surfs.

Whoosh! Waves lifted, and then pushed, the girls backwards. They landed onto a causeway flanked on either side by the wetlands. This was where the sprite had been. Helen and Sharon refocused their efforts on their magical guardian's path. They crawled toward the feline fairy who waited at the base of the Chromlechon. The causeway was dry and easier to traverse than the bogs.

Too tired and bruised to run, they limped with urgency.

The ground shook. Behind them, sorcerous waves clashed with belligerent demon babies. Showers of water wetted the departing children and muffled the babies' wails.

Now was not the time to linger or watch. The cat led them through a circuitous route networking up the porous mountain. Shuffling on bruised knees, peering with dark ringed eyes, they followed their guide to the warm Pyre.

Helen and Sharon's wet bodies collapsed before the fire. They lay upon warm stone staring at angelic flames. Vapors steamed away from their clothing. In front of them, their guide strutted with deliberation. Its mission complete, it bounded into the fire. Smoke and flame enveloped it. They had seen too many weird, irreconcilable events to think logically. Dangerous demons still preyed on them. Safety must lie ahead. Hope lay in that blaze.

The two friends stood on weary legs, held hands, and stepped into the fire…

IV: Wraith's Nest

" **G**RAVE, GET TO *the Pyre. A sprite returns.*"
    "Aye, Lord. I am there already and bear witness." The spirit of the paper-cat had grown as it mingled with that of the two girls it led. Its aura was a wild inferno so large that Grave was compelled to step away.

    Grime coated the children. The pelt of the white-haired one was matted with burrs and nettles; she held a mangled carcass. Her companion wore a thin muslin dress; she clenched a leather doll with glass eyes. Their spirits shielded that of the tiny wasps hidden inside their things.

    Lord Lysis strode in carrying two stone mutant-babies. A third grub-baby remained skewered on *Ferrus Eviscamir.* "Doctor, secure these."

    "Yes, Lord." The Doctor seemed dissatisfied. "I may be able to harvest the blood of one for experimentation. I will cage them for safe study," Doctor Grave concealed the bodies from the orphans. "Have you welcomed our newcomers?"

"Doctor, who are they? Their auras are almost unread-able." Their swollen eyes peered from atop puffy, blackened cheeks. They were close to joining his own daughters in death. They shrank back from Lysis. His empathy increased his angst.

Grave discerned their names and shrugged. "They repress much. Minds hide away such horrors for protection sometimes. They will go mad if they do not confront reality. In any event, they have reached physical safety now. The sprite has done its job. I will dismiss it."

Grave telepathically commanded the cat to jump into the Pyre. Rainbow flames enveloped it. Unaware of the sprite's origins, the girls stepped toward the heat to follow…

"No!" Lysis intervened, jumping in front of the orphans. The two fell backward, screaming. They were terrified, but no longer in danger of burning. "Do not fear me. I protect you."

Helen reached for the cat while Sharon wrapped her arms around her friend's waist and pulled. The pair staggered away from the skeletal warrior landing on their bottoms. Cowering within Lysis's shadow, exhausted of options, they gazed at the forbidding figure offering security. The girls sat quietly unable to understand their circumstances let alone act.

Grave drew near. "Lord, you save them from immediate threats, but not their haunting experiences. Differentiating you from the other demons they have faced will not be easy."

"Make yourself useful, Doctor. Convince them they are safe."

Grave addressed the girls. "What are your names?" Of course, the Doctor already knew their names, for their souls held echoes of 'Helen' and 'Sharon'. Verbalizing one's own identity was a test of a mind's health, but these two were too traumatized to respond.

OVER THE COMING days, all survivors were tasked to produce drawings. The Pyre transformed the donated art into beautiful, animated puppets sent to scour the countryside. Within a week, hundreds of orphans packed the Chromlechon corridors. Doctor Grave delegated responsibility to the eldest children to watch over other children.

Cecelia was one of several in charge. Her gifted torch from Lysis lashed in the air like a baton. "You there, stand in line. Hey, hey. hey. You three, in queue. Yes, there you go. Wait! Can't you see where I am pointing? Pick up the paper. Yes, now, follow the pointer. It is time to craft."

As therapeutic as creating art was, it was not enough to heal the young Keepers totally. Even Cecelia, who was one of the most responsive, suffered from tantrums. Helen and Sharon remained detached from the others. The two girls stayed near the Pyre. They did not pay attention to Cecelia, who had yet to recognize her sullen friend from Qual.

Grave reported his prognosis to Lysis. "The children are deeply unsettled. They calm when they make art. Schedules and common rules stabilize their behavior. Yet, they stay haunted. Those with toys sleep some. The others toss feverishly every night."

"We invited them here, Doctor. Shelter is not enough. We need to heal their minds, bring peace."

Doctor Grave professed, "You can either cut away memories as you did mine, to reduce the nightmares. Or you can repair what was lost. To do that, you will have to retrieve their past from where they lived."

Four animated rag-dolls emerged from the caves. Echo's puppets circled about Helen and Sharon. The Gray Foundling came last, clutching his one-armed doll and the skewered Aleece puppet.

"Doctor, Lord Echo's band of dolls gather."

"They play, Lord."

"No, they surround two children. Echo warns us."

At the center of the commotion, Sharon's doll began to wiggle. She took little notice of its movement. Blue larvae worked their way from deep within Lacey, sprinkling the ground. A score of ghostly insects burst out. Demonic wasps hovered in a thin cloud.

Lacey stood on her own accord, ensorcelled. Her leather dress swelled, stressing its silk ribbons and releasing cloth stuffing. Wasps escaped the seams. Her embroidered face showed no emotion, but her glass eyes glowed blue in the astral plane. The doll dug with her mitten-like hands, retrieving larvae from between her legs to throw on the cobblestone. Lacey's ghost yelled, *'Womb-ripper!'*

Lysis advanced, brandishing his sword. "It is possessed!"

Escaping the girl's weak arms, the doll ran haphazardly. Echo's white-eyed puppets gave chase. Lacey was caught, drawn, and nearly quartered by the four who pulled on each limb. Echo began to consume color from the target, working the ether with his mind. Several wasps fell from the sky as bits of stone, their blue depleted. The corrupted doll continued to writhe.

The Gray Foundling almost neutralized the menace himself. No longer seriously threatened, Lord Lysis reconsidered attacking with *Ferrus Eviscamir*. He spoke to Echo telepathically, *"Do not feed on this one. Let your puppets release it."*

The boy obeyed, trusting Lysis.

Freed, Lacey stepped back slowly, her eyes communicating the situation to a remote being. Whatever controlled the wasps also operated the doll. Lacey squatted while tugging at her belly. She yelled directly at Lysis, *"Where have you been, father? Ma is at home, caring for your sick children!"*

Lysis remained calm, unaffected by the wailing doll's accusations.

Meanwhile, Grave attempted to figure out who 'Ma' was. He combed through his sundered memories. Finally, he examined Lysis's aura to learn more about his lord's wife. *"If that represents your children, Ma would be…"*

Lysis ignored the golem. The fact that the Doctor could rekindle his memories was discomfiting.

"Rotten seed of the Lysis clan!" Lacey screamed, tossing luminescent larvae toward the Gray Lord.

Endenken Lysis sidestepped the grubs. He adjusted his grip on *Ferrus Eviscamir* drifting an even distance in a circular route, maintaining eye contact with Lacey. The possessed doll and skeletal warrior slowly switched places. Several larvae popped under Lysis's steps.

"You made us all sick, Womb-ripper! Follow me home where you can fix all your wrongs. Ma misses you."

The girls could not hear the doll's telepathic taunts issued on the astral plane, but they could see Lacey running around. Her animation reminded them of the mutant babies who chased them to the Keep, and the wasps reminded them of the dreadful fog about Qual. Confused, Helen cradled Spotty's lifeless form, squeezing it tighter and tighter. Suddenly she saw a blue glow on her hand. A wasp emerged from Spotty! She screamed and dropped the carcass. Horrified, Helen watched her dead cat regain its footing. Something had reanimated it—the same blue magic that had corrupted Lacey.

Possessed-Spotty stumbled toward Lacey. It limped awkwardly, eventually working out a consistent stride. It rubbed against the doll, which grabbed Spotty's fur and mounted it. Sharon's toy turned its head to Lysis again, *"How long do you seek to avoid us, father? Ma says to accept my invitation."*

The demonic pair went toward the precipice. They jumped over the parapet. No one else moved.

Suddenly Grave remembered. *"Maeve was your wife. My daughter?"*

"Yes, Doctor, but Maeve is *not* possessing the doll." Lysis, favoring his human origins, spoke aloud. Effigies of a brunette woman flared in his aura. "You will recall, when you relearn our full past, that she is gone. Forever gone."

Grave turned to Lysis. "Lord, Maeve's soul may be

gone, but memories of her remain."

"Maeve is not the issue here. I never fathered such dys-crasiac horrors. The doll's master is confused."

"Well, the reanimation and departure of those toys have left the girls confused too. Their minds will weaken without their security blankets."

"I will retrieve them," Lysis huffed. "I will also gather as many abandoned dolls as possible from Qual to help the others. First, I want those minions to lead me to their master. Otherwise, we will be plagued with more visitations. I must go find the source of the corruption. Tend to the children and their artisanal pyre, Doctor."

Grave spoke to his own master's departing backside, "Of course, Lord. A tedious task no doubt. To collect the toys, I suggest you encumber an elder ant with a supply wagon. There are some deserted below where the Gorgepath skirts the Chromlechon."

"Agreed. I will take the once-Queen."

Grave sighed. He did not mean to have his previous master enthralled so, having intended another of the once-Queen's brood to become animated.

"Must go." Echo repeated, looking over the rocks be-side his puppets. Lacey became a distant speck as it descended hundreds of yards onto scree. "Forever gone."

Lysis spoke. "Echo, you are Lord of the Chromlechon in my absence. Ensure the children are safe. Order the Doctor as you see fit."

The Gray Lords bowed slightly to bid farewell. Echo

then turned his head inquisitively toward Grave who indeed resembled a massive doll. "Puppet Doctor."

Grave watched Echo while reflecting on being a servant. The Doctor was subservient to Lord Lysis, of course, who controlled the ichor animating his body. Echo had animated puppets, yet those were simple constructs. The boy had never possessed a living creature. That day would surely come. If the boy were to mature into a true leader, he would have to learn to control bodies made by nature.

Echo slouched, and wiped glowing mucus from his nose onto his forearm.

L YSIS RODE THE once-Queen down the escarpment, gliding atop mounds of scree and bones, until the black lake surrounding the mountainous colony's base met him. The moat-like loch brimmed with brackish melancholy—a soulless humor. He crossed a skeletal causeway, which spanned across the wetland. Serpentine wyrms swam on either side; toxic gases bubbled around them. These were the ancient larvalwyrmen, part of the once-Queen's brood cursed to never mature. Lysis controlled them now.

Lacey meandered a hundred yards in front. Often, she rotated her head, laughed, and resumed. She welcomed the game, be it a hunt or play. She had, in fact, waited patiently for Lord Lysis to procure a cart to latch to the once-Queen. Now Lacey steered her undead, feline mount. She encouraged it to pounce on residual signatures left by the cat-sprite as they retraced its journey.

Having traversed the causeway and entered the country-side, the Lord engaged Lacey. *"Tell me. Don't you miss Sharon? You left her back at my Keep."*

"Ma tells me that Sharon was tricked. But you can't fool me."

"Sharon is safe now."

"She should come home. As you follow me now. To see Ma."

Lysis pushed for more, *"But—"*

"Hush, or I'm going to tell Ma that you are trying to hurt me. You should just talk to Ma."

Sunrise poured over the mountainous horizon. Nature was colorless, as far as the undead Lysis *saw*. Through crushed fields and burnt forests, he came upon a vast, ash-laden hillside. A pyroclastic flow had blasted through here. Now the once-Queen's legs shuffled through the dunes, stirring plumes and revealing smoldering embers. Yet she remained unharmed. Her chitin, as Lord Lysis's armor, was impermeable to heat.

The task at hand was to follow Lacey to its master. The doll trailed Helen and Sharon's footprints in the ash. The girls had entered Lysis's brother, SanGules' mansion, which had survived the cataclysm. If not for the valuable, if painful, memories of Maeve held within, the lord would have razed it already. Lacey did not linger here.

Three cats stalked the group. Their souls marked them as Spotty's enduring kin. Shadow and Smokey paused to stare at the procession of *daimones:* the once-Queen and the skeleton upon her back parading behind their undead sister. The tabby Queen-Bee, accompanied her two offspring on a hunt for Spotty. The cats' quest to reunite with a healthy Spotty, or to eliminate her if diseased, crossed with Lysis's mission. Queen-Bee had no desire to interfere with the Gray Lord's work. She and her living kittens would observe from the sideline for a time.

"This way to Qual, my Lord!" Lacey hollered.

It was not long until a woven barricade intersected the road. The construct resembled a beaver dam, ten yards tall and fifty yards wide. Qual dolls adorned the nest. Many had missing legs and arms. Tufts of stuffing breached these orifices.

"Ma says we need to free the dolls," Lacey conveyed.

The mounted Lysis looked around. "Beware. The owner of this nest arrives."

Three conjoined bodies rose from behind the heap. Its central avian head shrieked. Rhythmic clanking issued from the involuntary snapping tusks of its ant skull. A drooping, drooling human head remained still.

"Protect me!" Blue-Lacey pleaded as it jumped into the wagon bed. *"'tis a doll stealer. It will consume my soul!"*

The wraith leapt toward them. It circled the trespassers. Eyes locked on the Lord and the once-Queen. It saw two fellow white-bloods. It strafed while gazing with scrutiny, shocked to encounter the living, separated versions of itself. Then it detected blue fire within the wagon. Delicious cerulean energy! It squawked. Its twisted language uninterpretable.

Lysis communicated to Grave who remained in the

Chromlechon, *"Doctor. Echo's siblings, Cypria's brood, are here. One is attracted to Lacey. Why, Doctor?"*

"Because it is hungry for color, and the wasps inside the doll radiate energy."

After completing a second trip around the travelers, the wraith was taken off-step by a sudden strike. In a split second, the once-Queen lurched, sinking her elephantine pincers into either side. Her tusks lifted the flailing Gallwraith and held it aloft.

Spotty and Lacey were launched to the back of the wagon. Now bent over the rail, Lacey ranted, *"Womb-ripper! Your blood is the same. You are one of its kin!"*

"This creature is no ally of mine. This wraith is starving. I shall feed it." Lysis turned to thrust *Ferrus Eviscamir* toward Lacey, the blade's point skewering a wasp from her belly. The doll yelled as Lysis extended the tip to the suspended mutant. The wasp stopped thrashing as it turned to stone. He flicked his sword to remove it.

Lacey screeched, *"Child killer! You kill your own children!"*

"You, are no ally of mine either." Lysis turned back to the doll anticipating another retort. Instead, the ghostly visages of his eleven children stared at him. Confused, his memories were mingling with the power within the doll. *"Doctor, how many enemies do I face?"*

Grave responded via the ethereal tendrils connecting his blood to his master's heart, *"You encounter two enemies. The first is the dyscrasiac possessor of Lacey, whose identity remains a mystery. The other is the injured Gallwraith. It, like Echo, was spawned by Cypria. It bleeds eucrasiac* lapis elixir, *as you do. That thing is a* chromantis, *an ancient hybrid that the once-Queen feared."* Grave continued, *"It would be worthy to study alive. Can you retrieve it for me?"*

Lysis ignored the request. *Ferrus Eviscamir* carved. He targeted only chitin shell and bone flesh. As the body was hewn, the fleshy casing could not hold its contents. Blood let from every slice. "It does bleed *lapis elixir*. I freed it from Cypria's Gallwomb. Now I slay it.'

"Lord, although Gallwraiths are mutants, their blood is of the right balance, but their corporeal vessels are misshapen. They are not as well mixed as their sibling, the Foundling Echo. But spilling their blood is wasteful. It is valuable regardless of the source."

Indifferent, Lysis watched the blood drain onto the absorptive ash. *"Where is Lord Echo now, Doctor? I cannot reach his mind."*

BACK IN THE Chromlechon, Grave examined the insectan boy. Echo sat on the Dissection Theater's stage, head downcast, attempting to cover his globular eyes while keening and crying aloud: "Hungry, hungry, hungry."

The Gray Foundling slowed his rocking, his skin becoming harder and harder, crystallizing into a shell. Radiant ichor seeped from thin cracks. The more he solidified, the more he called out. Echo could no longer move his legs. Energy flowed from his audience to the young Lord.

Around the boy wavered his three favorite puppets: a fowl-wraith, a one-armed warrior, and an impaled woman. As Echo weakened, so did his control over them. They did not have the strength to stand anymore. They toppled into the pit beside the stage. They fell into the dark, abandoned nursery below.

"My Lord, Echo plays with his puppets." Lighting was dim in the Theater, since only one torch illuminated the vaulted chamber. Echo had accidentally drained his audience of energy. Fourteen children stood motionless in a semi-circle, still as statues in the cold auditorium—their eyes rolled up and backward, as if their pupils hid from watching the nightmare on stage though their bodies were compelled to face it. All irises were drained of color. Cecelia had become unresponsive. She held her bone-torch with a death grip. Her ginger hair was now striped like her hosiery: achromatic streaks ran through it.

Grave surmised that their lives could still be saved. Echo's outburst must have been localized to the stage.

"Hungry," Echo prattled.

Grave comforted him. "Worry not about your dolls. They remain unharmed. But your friends fare worse. You consumed their energy, Lord Echo. We must teach you to control your sorcery. You feed improperly."

"Doctor, are you listening to me?"

"Of course, Lord Lysis," Grave lied. *"The Foundling is fine. He is before me now. Know that your blood is not diseased like your ancestors were. Blue-blood is much more reactive.*

Have you found the source controlling the doll and cat?"

"T̲ʜ̲ᴇ̲ɪ̲ʀ̲ ̲ᴍ̲ᴀ̲s̲ᴛ̲ᴇ̲ʀ̲ ̲ʀ̲ᴇ̲s̲ɪ̲ᴅ̲ᴇ̲s̲ in *Qual.*" Lysis dismounted the once-Queen. As she kept the Gallwraith suspended to bleed out, he followed after Lacey, who had jumped from the wagon. The doll was inspecting four charred, adult corpses. Their souls burned dimly.

Lysis asked, *"Is this your Ma?"*

"No, silly. My Ma is your wife, *and she is not here."*

Lysis recognized signatures in the souls. He spoke to the ghosts. *"Can you communicate? I seek the parents of two girls."*

A female spirit spoke, *"The storm took them as it did us. Black clouds rolled in, crackling with lightning, spitting fire. They never made it inside. Can you find them, and lay their bodies next to ours?"*

Lord Lysis returned, *'Helen and Sharon outlive you. They are in my custody away from the damaged land.'*

'What do you need from us?' Helen's father asked.

'I seek to heal your daughters' minds. They need some of your memories.' Lysis sliced the air while speaking an eldritch language. *Ferrus Eviscamir* freed and absorbed ghostly recollections. He read the secrets he gathered. Helen had wandered into the fields as a toddler. Her parents searched to no avail. Days later, they awoke to scratching at the door. A cougar had brought their daughter home. "Helen has a guardian angel," her

father had said. Years transpired and the wild cat returned. They found it curled up dying of old age.

"I preserved her pelt for Helen. She called her Angie, short for 'angel'. Who looks over Helen since I am gone?"

Endenken Lysis said, *'I am her guardian now. She wears the pelt still, which I will renew with your spirit."*

Lady Nadeen's ghost interrupted. *"What about our daughter?"*

"Who are you, Lady? You are too regal to have lived in the countryside."

"Where is she? Where?" Nadeen responded. *"I knew this would happen. I told you, Don! I told you!"* Her astral presence became turbulent with anger, her voice difficult to interpret.

Lysis turned to the husband whose soul was calmer.

Lord Donquasen explained, his burnt, tailored clothes marked him a textile expert. *"My wife and I came here to examine a new dyeing process. Our home is... was... in the district center. I was to be regent in the Clanlord's absence. I had thought it safe enough to venture out. Nadeen was less sure. Sharon was playing with Helen when the storm came."*

"Fear not. Sharon lives and is also under my care."

Relieved, Donquasen asked, *"Can you find our Clanlord? Save Qual?"*

"Urlqualenson died in battle, as did his son. I work to secure a future for your children away from the city. Many are at my keep without their toys. I seek to gather and return as many dolls as I can."

Lacey disrupted the scene. *"Oh no, you want to steal us!"*

"Lacey!" Lord Don's ghost recognized the doll.

Lysis aimed *Eviscamir,* *"Beware, she is corrupted."*

"You steal from your own kin," the doll accused.

"No, Lacey. We will collect the dolls and bring them back to your mother."

"Ooh, she will be so excited!"

Lysis and Lacey extracted three score dolls from the nest and piled them in the wagon. Lysis also gathered Helen and Sharon's parents. He was unsure where to bury them, but leaving them here was not right. The once-Queen's wagon was nearly full. Peering over the barrier, Lysis looked in disgust at the many unhatched eggs. *"Doctor, there is a whole nest of mutants here. I will eliminate them."*

"You could save them to study."

"You sympathize with these creatures too much," Lysis growled.

"Lord, if they were corrupted humans, *would you ex-ecute them?"*

Lysis vaulted into the nest. *"These things have no hu-manity in them."* He cut through the shells with ease. Each slice of *Ferrus Eviscamir* released great plumes of atomized ichor. Prismatic splashes sprayed the air. Every egg was destroyed. The whole nest burned with pearly flames as the energy within the *lapis elixir* was released. Lord Endenken Lysis's soul burned bright. Satisfied with his work, he mounted the once-Queen beyond the astral-inferno's reach.

"*So we go home now? Or are you going to steal us back to the mountain?*" Lacey whined. "*Ma says you feel guilty about coming home. She says it's your fault she fell ill. Your seed was rotten. Then you abandoned us.*"

Lysis spoke to Lacey. "*I will go home now.*"

"*Ma will be so happy!*"

"*Take me then. Lacey, lead me to my wife.*" They went along the overgrown Gorgepath toward Qual City. "*Doctor, the possessed doll leads me to its master.*"

V: Ghosts' Manor

"**D**OCTOR, SOMETHING IS *amiss,*" Lysis mindspoke as he entered Qual's territory. Stunted humanoids stalked him away from the road, hiding in fields of poppy, lily, and flax. These shadowy entities maintained anonymity via distance. Each was no taller than a fox. Lysis could not confirm if they were foes ready to set ambush, survivors seeking help, or both.

"*How so, Lord?*" Grave sat on the edge of the Theater's stage as his lord's surroundings filled his mind.

No palisade surrounded Clan Qual. Its hub was not a fortress as was the case for Clan Lysis, or a walled city as was Clan Tonn. This was an open district and its central governance had run from a three-storied, two-winged mansion. For miles about the manse, rolling hills had harbored livestock and vegetation supporting their trade. Now, confused sheep meandered about the desolate hills hunting for scarce milkweed or clover. Decaying livestock and fence posts were partially submerged like flotsam on an ocean of cooled ash. Meadows smoldered underneath, giving rise to hundreds of miniature, active chimneys. Banks of charnel powder grew deeper and deeper as Lysis approached the city center. Dust collected alongside the western side of the architecture. Powdery drifts formed great arabesque curls against all dwellings. Smokestacks and thatched roofs barely reached above the drifts.

All was gray except for the glowing wasps that hovered about. Any color the undead Lord could *see* was incorporeal. Luminous blue honeycombs grew atop dilapidated structures. Phantom figures lined the abandoned road.

Lord Lysis observed the entombed town's many buildings that burned ethereal fires. *"There is movement in the shadows. Looks like children dancing in front of candles. Perhaps some sought refuge inside the ruins."*

"If there are living urchins, they will eventually follow you, Lord. Leave them for now. First remove the evil that possess their land. Follow Lacey to its master spirit."

Lysis rode in line with roof tops above the buried boulevard. It was if the once-Queen floated upon the snow-swept arctic. Foot-long knitting needles were set along the path to the Clanlord's manor. *Atop* the ash. These recently-impaled pieces of paper were his pyre-sprites.

"Dyscrasiac creatures roam here. They evolved after the opening of Cypria," Lysis determined. *"They neutralized our invitations."*

Blue-Lacey cried out, *"Worry not about those paper creatures, my Lord."* The doll leaned from Spotty to retrieve a metal skewer. Lacey held it aloft as a baton and pointed forward.

Fragments of burned vellum broke free. *"We children of Qual are not scared of these alien magics. But beware, they reek of poison. Ma does not like them."*

They strode atop a submerged bazaar. Apparitions of it were visible only to the dead. Lord Lysis analyzed the ghosts. Their visages were dilated and stretched by the pyroclastic rock in which they were encased. Therein were petrified humans clustered within the apothecary market, a center of commerce, which brought merchants from afar. Tonn sculptors and jewelers were stationed in rows showcasing glass eyes and metallic pigments from their mines. Liveried clothiers and drapers local to Qual sold linens. Lord Qualenson, master tailor, and his son Urlquason anointed dolls ceremoniously—all children within Qualenson's district were supplied such a figurine, usually manufactured by the parents with materials associated with the family's craft.

"Who rules a district when the lord is absent?" Lysis reflected. He asked the escort doll, "Who is your master? Who controls you?"

Lacey led Lysis through the rooftops, a dozen feet atop the layered cobble. *"We take you to Ma now."* Lacey waved her wand of deceased Pyre-sprites, *"My invited guest, come. Come!"* Larvae occasionally dripped out of her opened seams.

As if attracted to the strewn maggots, pairs of glowing eyes rapidly appeared in second floor windows. Astral shadows flickered as wasp-animated dolls clambered through broken panes. Shards tore through stretched fabric. Undaunted, they proceeded. Those freed from the houses ran onto the boulevard, collecting larvae as if it was prized candy. Many arrived waving ribbons strung from wands. More came brandishing garland made from Lysis's colorless sprites.

Cartwheeling toward them came a whirling sock puppet. A pink blur comprised of rotating red and white stripes. This was Cecelia's doll Bailey. His legs and arms were made from knee-length hosiery. His head was disproportionately shaped, being as thin as the torso from which it budded, and no wider than the appendages. He was firmly stuffed with buckwheat husk and infested with blue-larvae. His yarn hair had all but fallen out. His glass eyes were lost, so two vacancies with stray strands enabled larvae to egress. His mouth was stitched shut. Bailey's lengthy stride carried him beside Spotty and his old playmate Lacey.

Lysis looked into the wagon bed to check the dolls he had retrieved from the wraith's nest. They were now possessed, animated, by a sorceress 'mother'. These puppets sprung overboard and celebrated as if freed from prison. He allowed the dolls to depart, but would not let the wasps defile the parents of Helen and Sharon. He cast a spell to ward off the insects from those corpses. The dolls he could always gather again after dealing with the master of this charade.

Yard by yard, the parade intensified. Dolls trailed Lysis with strands of rope, occasionally crisscrossing to subtly weave a fabric cage. Sets of five came streaming out with billowing sheets in tow. Plush toys hung from nooses, held aloft on loom battens. Tufts of stuffing puffed out as the dolls bearing them danced in the macabre procession. Improvised music erupted all around as the gaieties reached a crescendo. Piss-pots were drummed upon, as were circular knitting looms strung with leather heads, while cow bells rang and wind chimes jingled. The discordance echoed across the desolation.

"Doctor, I have found more dolls. The parading puppets attempt fanfare."

"Clan Qual was not known for music," Grave commented.

To the doll, Lysis said, *"I look forward to meeting your mother. Where is she?"*

"Lord womb-ripper, Ma is where you left her!" Lacey decried, *"Lady Sabina awaits you in the mansion!"*

"Doctor, the possessor of Lacey is mad. It thinks I am one of my ancestors. A witch named Sabina *is in charge."*

"Ah, the wife of Lord Derryk Lysis," Grave said, *"One of your great grandfather's three sons. The eldest."*

Lysis replied, *"I recall he was a basket weaver, an osier who had taken wives from Tonn, Qual, and the Chromlechon. Each of his wives died while pregnant, infested with dyscrasia. His plight was one of the prime examples taught in our family. Mating outside the clan triggered mutations, as you had warned us. Derryk eventually came home to Gravenstyne and hung himself. His ghost swings beside my son Atalen on the same beam. You had tended to my clan's funerals before I was born, tell me where he was buried."*

"Derryk's body lies in Gravenstyne's catacombs. No doubt Lacey leads you to the Qual manor house to see Lady Sabina, his second wife. Masquerade as her husband to get

close," advised Grave.

The cavalcade bloomed as thousands of wasps surged onto the main street. Light from the silver moon paled, in comparison. Emotionally, the tone grew darker, since living humans were brought into the fray. A girl shrouded in snow-white fleece was led by her hair. An orphaned boy was pulled from a chimney by his feet, his chin slicing open as it scraped brick. Others came covered in sheets dressed as ghosts.

Sabina's minions were controlling dead bodies too. Lysis saw one burial place open up, and then another, and another. Women's and men's corpses were exhumed and ushered forth by possessed dolls. Lysis kept his composure atop the once-Queen as he analyzed the souls of the disinterred. None were spared humiliation: young and old; poor and rich; modest and proud. Representatives from all walks of life were haphazardly decorated with rags, frilled gowns, and shrouds. With the tempo of the music, the dolls waggled and wriggled the bodies as if the corpses were puppets. Beat after beat, the dead clowns danced. The rattle and clatter of the reanimated ensured that none rested in peace.

The parade took special care of dead youths. The dolls wrapped these into cocoons, raised them high, as pallbearers would raise coffins, and then they sang:

"Aloft the children go,
And we say so and we hope so.
We'll hoist them up and bury them low.
O, poor old Lord!

We say, old Lord, your wife will rise,
And we say so and we hope so.
O, poor old Lord your wife will rise,
O, poor old Lord!"

"Doctor, the witch Sabina has her dolls collect children.
I need to free the orphans, but they are captured by the very toys
that I also need to rescue. I cannot hurt that which I came to
collect," Lysis placed his hand on *Eviscamir's* hilt. *"How can*
I fight them?"

Marshalling the procession, Lacey directed Lysis to the fore. *"Lord Derryk, your sword won't help you. It is worthless here. And your attire is not suitable for the grand union that awaits. You need royal dress. You, master weaver, deserve an osier's crown!"* With a wave of her wand, Lacey ordered Sabina's other minions to present Lord Lysis with a coronet of weeping willow branches. He placed it on his antlered head. Then a long mantled, royal vestment was thrown over his shoulders. It was a tapestry embroidered with Derryk's name taken from their Clanlord's manor.

Lacey exclaimed, *"All hail, Lord Derryk Lysis, husband to our Lady Sabina! Welcome our guest of honor!"*

Doctor Grave responded, *"Do not engage yet. Stay focused on reaching Sabina. Maintain the ruse."*

Hundreds of animated dolls cheered. Clouds congested the sky, suffocating the moon's luster. The land of the living grew darker, and by contrast, the astral signatures of memories and ghosts grew brighter.

Finally, Qualenson's manse could be seen. A quarter mile to the northwest, it burned as an azure inferno. Its third floor emerged from the frozen dunes. Before it, the collapsed coach house lay under a mass of entangled, petrified horses. A dozen canopied carriages intermixed with the convoluted heap.

The landscape appeared covered in a wrinkled drapery. Smooth waves of igneous rock covered the estate's arbors, gardens, and *allée* walkways. Small lakes were completely buried. The willow trees surrounding them looked like small bushes. Three ghosts of stillborn children haunted these; the bodies had hung as ornaments for years but were missing now. *The demonic babies who chased Helen and Sharon to my Keep came from here,* Lysis realized. *They were Derryk's babies, hung by his own hand.*

Lacey looked backward as Spotty picked up pace. Bailey ran alongside with an exaggerated stride afforded by gangly, sock legs. Lacey yelled, *"Come, father womb-ripper! Welcome home."*

'Womb-ripper' resonated with Lysis. He was not sure why Sabina labelled Derryk that. Perhaps it was due to her cursed impregnations. In any event, Endenken Lysis could also be called such for splitting Cypria's Gallwomb. That cataclysmic event birthed Echo, and then ruined all to the west of the Gallwomb with a ground-hugging avalanche of scalding pumice. The mansion was affected by a quake that preceded the pyroclastic flow, evidenced by the shift in the west wing's foundation. Its roof angled incongruously, a full yard higher than the level east wing.

"This way!" Lacey hailed, spurring Spotty into a gallop toward the eastern wing of Qualenson's chateau. The dormers of the south-facing third floor were largely intact, each appearing as an entry threshold. Carved gargoyles extended from each and supported glowing, honeycombed nests. Some window panes had cracked. The undead cat jumped through a breach. The pallbearing dolls trailed, holding cocooned children overhead. The once-Queen was too large to fit. Lysis dismounted and followed alone.

Outside, the remaining parade turned mischievous. Having reached their destination, the crowd kept circulating, transferring its momentum into curling spirals. Concentric rings of dancers rotated like cogwheels. Marching in layers, dolls holding rope subtly wove a grand net around the eldritch ant. Puppets armed with needle lances patrolled on undead sheep. They celebrated the homecoming of Lord Derryk, and they awaited orders from their master, Lady Sabina.

SPOTTY DARTED DOWN the bland corridor of the servant quarters, descended a tight stairwell, and emptied onto a balcony overlooking a great room. The gallery was two stories high. Displayed on the interior wall were gonfalons of the three primary clans emblazoned with heraldry designed by the master of Qual. Lysis noticed Clan Tonn's white silhouettes of rampant wyverns as well as Clan Qual's ermine standard before settling a serious gaze on his own clan's coat of arms. Clan Lysis's shield was decorated per bend sinister, principally charged with one heart and three drops of blood; the coat of arms was helmed with an apple tree, supported by wasps; the motto read: 'Legacy and Melancholy.' He brooded for an instant to Grave. *"My legacy has been determined. I destroyed my ancestors because they were diseased. I overcame my clan, its muse, your Queen. Then lost my wife to melancholy. Without any living heirs, no one else should be as cursed. Yet dyscrasia haunts the land. Worse, I see that my ancestors were the cause of this relapse. Derryk the Osier corrupted the Lady Sabina."*

Spotty pranced down another set of stairs decked with a marble balustrade, bounding onto what had been the original ground level. Then the cat raced into the adjacent Hall of Mirrors. The showroom displayed the clan's *haute couture*. Here fashion was prominent whether a visitor was shopping, studying the art of tailoring, or socializing. Blank-faced statues served as dress forms. They were stationed throughout the tiled floor donning intricately laced gowns, pleated pannier, and black laced dresses.

Sunlight once showered the room from the south, sparkling the gilded trim, the mirrors opposite, and the dangling chandeliers. Now, only unnatural light illuminated the submerged mansion, namely, from the appalling glow of scurrying wasps. Psychotropic memories shone from the mirrors. Historic masquerades replayed continuously. Ostentatious monarchs, drunk on wine, swaggered. Sycophantic laughter reverberated harmoniously with a viol trio's allegro tempo.

Central to the room was a dormant, hexagonal fountain. Prior to the cataclysmic storm ruining the countryside, water sprayed a pair of statues at its center: a man and woman, back to back, each with arms outstretched holding a single stole in exultancy. The marble couple had been knocked from their pedestal. Their feet were raised high, their torsos balanced atop the lower wall. The woman's decapitated head smiled toward the ceiling. The unifying scarf was fractured now. The man's severed hands stubbornly held a portion of it. The fountain was absolutely dry now and encrusted with verdigris crystals. Sparkling, vaporous ether filled the basin reflecting the past, as did the mirrors on the exterior walls of the Hall.

Lysis looked into those mirrors' endless depths. A balding lord looked back. He was dressed less flamboyantly than all the others, as if a visitor from a different clan. Metal pins of apples and wasps on his cuffs presented his family's coat of arms. *Was that me?* A floral parasol spun beside him from a lady whose back faced the mirror. She lowered the umbrella, curtsied to the lord, and they began a formal dance. They maintained a few feet between them, circling. She had black, lustrous hair. *Was that Meave?* No, Endenken and Maeve had never been here. These astral projections could not be his memories—rather, these were past events. Another Lysis clan member and his wife from Qual was here.

Still looking into the mirror, Lysis saw a girl hiding behind one of the armatures. She peered slowly, then hid. She revealed herself again, slyly looking around. Then she pulled

the manikin's dress before her own waist as if she were trying it on. Lysis inspected the current chamber. This ghost only
inhabited the mirror.

"*No time to dally. Ma wants to see you,*" Lacey said.
"*She has waited such a long time.*"

Lysis resumed his chase as Lacey took off. Last in the
line of great rooms, capping the end of the west wing, was
a theater. Polished pews and ample lighting set it apart from
the Chromlechon's operating theater, but it appeared equally
haunted. A mountain of needles had been collected on the stage.
Possessed dolls played on it, skewering one another with pins,
as if sword fighting. Aggressive puppets clambered to the top
and attempted to maintain control. Gentler dolls sewed the bodies of their brethren, sent them back to play. Behind the stage, a
grand staircase led to the basement. Lacey led her guest down
toward Lady Sabina's crypt. A procession of deceased children
followed.

They reversed trajectory in the basement stairwell, turning to head east. This was a long corridor running the length of
the entire mansion. They traversed a storeroom: bolts of cloth,
tartan hides, and furs, and large equipment such as dyeing vats
and industrial warp looms. A stash of glass eyes and rhinestones
crafted by Clan Tonn was stockpiled here. Under the central
foyer, the foundation had cracked. A crevice spanning a foot's
width separated the East Wing from the main hub.

Wasps swarmed the end of the hallway. The procession
was at a close. Sabina's dolls loaded the silk-wrapped children
into empty niches. The children looked like pupae curled up in

honeycombs. Wasps burrowed into the bodies. Still the pall-bearers sang:

> *"For many days you've hidden her,*
> *And you'll know, and we'll say so.*
> *And when she rises, she'll mother again,*
> *O, poor old Lord!*
>
> *And when mother rises, she'll mother again,*
> *And you'll know, and we'll say so.*
> *She'll raise the children with tighter rein,*
> *O, poor old Lord!"*

Around the bend, Lacey led Lord Lysis into the Portrait Hall, the hallway of royal crypts. Between each sealed vault, the walls were curtained with the clan's heraldic ermine signature, inversed such that the background field was dark sable and the patterns gilded. The designs were an abstract representation of fur, and by design, these mourning pennants were framed with real hide. The ruined corridor had buckled, cracked walls, some of which had collapsed to tear the tapestries.

Just as the Lysis Clan had done in Gravenstyne Fortress, Clan Qual buried their dead below ground and honored their ancestors with portraiture. Each vault's threshold displayed a woven effigy of the deceased made from its threaded hair and skin. Notably absent were those of Derryk and Sabina. Their deaths were not traditional. Derryk was not even entombed here, having been exiled from Qual as she was interred. Sabina was buried alive while diseased.

"Doctor Grave, I go to our woman of interest. Lady Sabina's crypt is before me."

"Good, Lord. Control her heart and all her minions

shall be yours. If you can take it subtly, then you can avoid harming the dolls."

"*Come on!*" Lacey yelled, poking her head from inside the breach. "*Ma expects you.*"

VI: Lady's Crypt

THE CRYPT'S THRESHOLD had been damaged in the quake that issued upon the opening of Cypria's Gallwomb. Wasps flew in and out of the breach. Lysis read the inscription on the cracked marble panel: "Here lies Lady Sabina, wife to Osier Derryk Lysis. Buried alive in her eighth month of her second pregnancy, whence her water broke and illness crawled forth. Condemned: Dyscrasia."

Lacey hopped off Spotty, climbed through the broken threshold, and clambered onto Sabina's lap. Her ghostly voice echoed from inside, *"I brought him home, Ma! Just as you told me. The dolls too."*

Bailey took a stance at Sabina's feet as if a butler.

Endenken Lysis entered what appeared to be a welcoming parlor. Heavy curtains decorated with *fleur de lis* patterns donned the walls. Frilled pennants traced the ceiling. A crowd of dolls crawled atop woven baskets at the base of a stone dais. Lady Sabina's back was toward him. A parasol twirling over her left shoulder blocked her from sight. An intense blue aura silhouetted her body as she sat awkwardly astride a closed, marble sarcophagus. She could not turn, given that her shackled legs were sprawled apart and anchored to the floor.

Four cowled statues held her. Doctor Grave's ethereal signature hovered around these. He and his Guild of Barbers had sealed her in.

"Derryk?" Sabina's ghostly voice resonated, filled with longing, wonder, and resentment. "Are you here?"

"Yes, my Lady." The undead warrior shuffled slowly around her side, halting before facing her. Wasps crawled on her alabaster thighs, scurrying frenetically, disappearing between them. Lysis had to navigate the statues. He touched the sculpted folds of their frozen robes. These men had been living once, serving the guild in the Chromlechon's Dissection Theater.

"I found Lady Sabina, Doctor Grave. She is shackled by four beings dressed as you." Two on either side had held her arms, but leaned away having lost their grip. They seem to have been solidified while swatting the air. The other two robed men had knelt to brace her shackled feet on either side of the marble. Amazingly, Sabina had remained animated. *"I did not expect to see your signature here. Tell me, Doctor, why do I see your minions of old here, cast in stone?"*

Grave contemplated alchemical petrification, since Echo, who now stood near, was similarly frozen. The Gray Foundling was perfectly stationary, his outer self a hard shell. Children deposited art by Echo's feet in memorial, as if he had died. The Doctor responded via telepathy, *"Mutations always occurred whenever your clan mated outside of your bloodline. My Guild of Barbers monitored every birth. Lady Sabina's previous pregnancy resulted in three stillborn mutants. This time, Sabina's womb had developed into a hive. We had attempted to bring the babies to term, despite her dyscrasiac infection. Her offspring came early. My doctors transmuted into stone when they were stung. I had to seal them in with her."*

Lysis did not know of Echo's status but sensed Grave was hiding something. *"What compels you, Doctor?"*

"As ever, I serve family. At the time of Sabina's internment, my master was Haemarr, last of the once-Queen's brood. We studied dyscrasia as it consumed our colony." As the Doctor communicated, children of the Chromlechon crowded around him with drawings, painted scrolls, and sculptures of folded paper. He gestured them away from Echo and toward the Pyre. Still, most children did not understand. They waited for verbal commands by his side holding their offerings.

"You serve me now."

"Yes. You and Lord Echo."

"And how fares Echo?"

The Doctor held a vial of smelling salt to wake Cecelia, who had struggled to remain conscious ever since Echo's uncontrolled consumption. Grave opened the vial of salt crystals beneath her nose. Pungent vapors of *sal ammoniac* infiltrated her brain, tugged her from a protective slumber. Her eyes opened wide. Light-headed, she did not stand. The doctor then awoke the others that had been adversely affected by Echo's untamed sorcery. *"Worry not, Lord Lysis. Echo is still entertaining in the Theater. All the children are sustaining the Pyre. In your absence, we are adding order to the Keep."* Grave motioned for the waiting children to sit. Those orphans who already donated their creative works looked pale. Many felt faint and collapsed. Some he propped near the Pyre to rejuvenate. All the while, Grave calculated responses to his Lord. *"The children desperately need what you seek. Collect their dolls with haste. You must destroy the witch who controls them."*

Sabina's back remained turned to him. But her hair was plain to see. It resembled Maeve's curly, black locks. Lysis grew distracted, increasingly reluctant to walk one more step to face the woman before him. Many dolls ran about Lysis now. Memories of his children's spirits chased the puppets. Phantom calls from his girls and boys echoed in the ether. Their laughter pulsed with his heartbeat.

His hallucinations were eclipsed by Sabina's trembling voice, "Are you afraid to see me?"

Lysis noticed her bare shoulders showing through the gown. Dark blue veins spread within her translucent porcelain skin. Maeve's flesh had been similar, though her blood had been darker. "No. I just pause in wonder, my Lady. And shame. You may not recognize me. Life has not treated me well."

"Nor me. Come around from behind. Delay fate no longer. Face me as we both desire."

He edged toward Lady Sabina's front side. Her evening gown was fitting of a Lady of Qual. Her bodice comprised criss-crossing brocade woven with pink and green silk, resembling peacock feathers. The evening ensemble was adorned with rhinestone-studded ruffles. Curling nails extended from her skeletal fingers. They were like polished sapphire. Her crotch and belly were rent open. Skin flapped aside. Luminous blue honeycombs grew in the cavity of her empty womb. Wasps and larvae crawled everywhere. Lacey sat in Sabina's lap, playing with the insects. Sabina's heart glowed azure through her translucent skin. Coiffured ebony hair, braided in complex weaves, framed her gaunt face.

Conversely, she drank in his appearance. The lord before her was mantled in royal garments, embroidered with her husband's name. His aura stank of the Lysis clan. The willow he once crafted now crowned his head. Yet he had antlers in place of hair. And no skin. "Derryk, dyscrasia has indeed changed you."

"Yes, dear. It seems the benefit of the disease is a life enduring past death. You survived better. You look stunning. How did you keep your beauty?"

"So, I look preserved? My beauty has been protected in this cell." She stared at him. "Why did you let them bury me alive?"

"I did not let them, love. I resisted," Lysis pretended. "But the Chromlechon Barbers hauled me away as they sealed you in. Your family blamed me for your disease and banished me. Rightly so. I went back to Gravenstyne." Lysis collapsed to his knees. "Dyscrasia affected us during your first pregnancy. Recall? I had hung our three lifeless boys in the willow trees, since legends said they may be revived. I thought they only needed time to mature. But they never awoke. After you were interred while pregnant again, our first children began to haunt me. Their ghosts started to follow me... telling me to come back for you. But you had been sealed here. I did not know the crypt was cracked open until Lacey invited me back."

The act placated her. Sabina began to beautify her hair with her overgrown fingernails, primping and twirling her tresses. She also twiddled her earrings, glancing nervously at the animated dolls playing atop the baskets. Minute larvae dripped out of her eye sockets, like tears. Mouth agape, she did not seem to care about being so infected. She continually monitored her dolls. Some climbed upon her lap, around her open womb. Two wasp-ridden dolls attempted to nurse on her breasts. Others played chaotically. Sabina's soul made it clear: even as one undead, she desired to be a homemaker. She was obsessed with attending to her offspring.

"Give 'em to me!" the aura of a ponytailed doll yelled.

A bald, masculine doll ran away with a needle in hand.

The feminine one gave chase. *"I said give 'em up!"*

"Take 'em if you want 'em." The instigator halted, turned abruptly, and skewered the one who chased.

Sabina ordered, "Stop piercing your sister! You there, give her back her eyes. Listen to Ma!" Without ensuring the orders were obeyed, Sabina gave her attention to Lacey who tugged on her hair.

"Ma," Lacey spoke to her ear, her aura reddened with mischief. *"I have something to tell you. Listen—"*

"Not now, dear, I want to talk to your Lord Derryk," Sabina petted Lacey. To her husband she asked, "Do you like our children?"

"Children? I see none."

"The wasps. This colony is ours. I, their mother queen, you their father."

"Why possess the dolls?"

"They are discarded tokens of Qual. Our children deserve heirlooms, don't they?" She lowered her parasol to welcome the mass of dolls about her. She combed one's hair with her fingernails.

Lysis pondered, *She wants me to hug them. I need to get closer.* Her heart glowed from within her ribcage.

"Seize her heart, Lord, and all her colony will be nullified." Grave rallied his will.

"I shall be a good father, now that I have returned home." Kneeling beside Sabina, Lysis's energy drained. His own memories of Maeve surged from his soul's reclusive depths. He sincerely missed his own children. His warrior façade could only hide his angst for so long. He sympathized with Sabina. He looked up at her and saw Maeve instead. He looked away, only to *see* some of his own children playing around him: Karylyn, Veralyn, and Marilyn played tea… three of his boys' ghosts played hide-and-seek.

"You need no longer mourn, husband. We are together again. Stay with me. Let me touch you."

He obeyed, collapsing onto her infested lap. He said, "It's has been so long."

She hugged Lysis, kissed his head, and caressed his back. Chains rattled as she attempted to move off the sarcophagus to no avail, her legs still pinned to the dais. Lysis's head lay against the open womb. It was more hive than belly now. Her blue ichor ran through the honeycombs containing maturing pupae. Her heart was close. It beat faster and faster. She had hope now to leave this cell and grow her family. She had earnestly missed her husband. She loved her children, her human stillborn as well as her inhuman insects and the dolls they occupied.

Lysis pleaded, *"Help me, Doctor. Can you hear me?"*

In the Chromlechon Theater, Grave still tended to the petrified Echo. *"Yes, Lord. Why? Is Sabina threatening you?"*

"No. That is the problem. I am close. I see her heart within reach. She is passive."

"Then remove it. She is no better than the Gallwraiths. She is monstrous."

"No, her heart is filled with compassion. Can I not heal her? In fact, I do not think it is Sabina. I think that... she is Maeve returned..."

"You are enthralled. Sabina's blood is ill. Her colony infests the countryside. Sabina is dangerous." Grave confirmed coldly. *"She cannot be sane enough to cast a spell. I deem you weaken yourself."* The golem continued to examine Gray Echo, gently prodding the stone shell of the juvenile lord. In this, the Doctor's action mirrored Sabina's stroking of Endenken Lysis's back.

"Now, free me from these shackles," Sabina pleaded. "Free me from this crypt." She let Lysis rise.

He focused intently on her ankles. *"Grave, these are warded manacles. How can I reverse your spells cast long ago?"*

"Lord, are you testing my loyalty? You need to end her."

"She is... just a mother... she is like Maeve. I must set her free."

"You need to free yourself. Use the sword to take her heart, Lord. Act now! Trust me, other than your memories of her, Maeve's life, soul, and body are utterly irretrievable. You should see only Sabina. And you must end her," Grave said.

Eleven dolls hugged Lysis then, and in each, one of his offspring's phantoms did embody: Gurylen, Olyen, Darilys, Kyrnelen, Veralyn, Marlyn, Evelyn, Addelyn, Karylyn, Atelen, Erolen. Hand in hand, they formed a ghostly circle. It was time to play. They rotated while singing:

> *"Four and twenty blackbirds*
> *Fail to say a word*
> *Ashes! Ashes!*
> *We all will burn!"*

Lysis spoke to them, "I failed you all. I am so sorry. Never again. I let you die." Then he telepathed to the Doctor, *"Grave, I see her. Maeve is alive! She is here. Trust me."*

To Sabina he said, "I can free you with my sword." He stood, raised *Ferrus Eviscamir,* and struck the shackles. Sparks flew. Sabina turned her head, anxious to be free but afraid Derryk would slice her feet off. Again and again he slashed. Winged minions fell with each swath, but the iron cuffs remained intact.

"Your weapon is killing our children!" Lady Sabina frantically tried to escape her chains. "What are you doing?"

Ferrus Eviscamir could not cut through the chains in its

current state. *"Tell me, Doctor. What are these shackles made of? How do I reverse your spell? I must free Maeve."* Lysis issued a pulsing shock through his own ichor pumping the golem doctor's heart. Grave trembled. *"Heed me, Doctor, I will end you if you do not obey me."*

"As you desire." Grave paused, decided, and then answered, *"To cut the manacles only, not bone or flesh, and to negate my old spell, you must recite another. Repeat this ancient speech as I tell it to you. Then say aloud the promise written on the hilt."* The Doctor spoke archaic expressions which Lysis recited, and the magical blade forged by the golem flared.

Finally, Endenken Lysis offered, "Queen, with this I will heal you." *Ferrus Eviscamir* struck out. The blade sliced through his own astral fire, crystallized his memories, and shattered them. The heads of his phantom children turned to glass as he cut them off. Ten decapitated corpses stood beside him. He no longer recognized them.

Sabina shouted, "I see your aura. You had other children. Healthy ones. You killed them?"

"My blade cuts my past too." Lysis dropped his sword. *"I'm stopping the spell! You tricked me Doctor."*

"Nay, Lord. As you helped me focus by cutting away my emotional ties to the once-Queen, you must continue to cut away your feelings. The past can confuse us. You would do less self-harm if your memories were extricated." Doctor solemnly replied. *"You must continue to cut."*

Endenken Lysis stood in shock. Sabina's minion puppets mobbed him. All he saw was dead children. He failed to save them. Were they his? He remembered one by name.

"Daddy?" Erolen's ghost pleaded from a ragdoll where Lacey was just standing. *"I ate the pear, Daddy!"*

Once-Spotty meandered about as Lacey tattletaled. *"Ma, he is not as he seems. He hoards our toys in his mountain. Steals from us,"* Lacey chimed in, *"Womb-ripper is a thief!"*

"Derryk, what is Lacey talking about?"

"Maeve, it is me." Lysis bent to hug Sabina. He stared at her face while on his side. "You've been gone, taken from me."

"Who is Maeve?" Sabina compared Endenken's spirit to the aura of the baskets around her. They had been crafted by Lord Derryk. Her husband's signature was slightly different than that of the twisted man before her. This being was from the same family. Yet this man was not her Derryk. "Imposter!"

"I tried to tell you something wasn't right, Ma!" Lacey exclaimed.

"Erolen, I won't hurt you again..."

"You Lysis folk are all poisonous." Lady Sabina spat, raising the parasol as if to strike. "I was buried alive because of your ill seed! I can read your intentions now. You are in league with the Barbers. You come to steal away Qualenson's dolls! Who are you, Deceiver?" She then ordered her minions, "Stop this thief!"

The crowd of dolls advanced. Lacey whisked away *Ferrus Eviscamir.* The blade proved too heavy for the meager doll. It tumbled to the floor.

"Children. Free me while I restrain him." Lady Sabina hugged her false suitor tight. The skeletal warrior trembled with cerebral fever rather than fighting her. Meanwhile, a dozen of her cloth minions came together to lift *Ferrus Eviscamir's* hilt. Playful, and uncoordinated, the assembly swung. The weapon slashed to and fro, its trailing aura poisoning all wasps. The dolls grew weaker and weaker as its power leached color from all that was astral-blue. "Careful, boys and girls! Aim at the shackles."

"Ma, the handle is very cold. It burns!" Lacey cried.

"Quickly, then," Sabina ordered.

Strength was not needed, just intent and proximity. The blade forged under Grave's hand reacted with the manacles likewise created by the golem. Electricity arced between surfaces. Black smoke churned in the air. The cuffs transformed from iron to glass, fractured, then crumbled.

Lady Sabina worked her way from under the heavy, distraught imposter. Her legs failed her. Collapsing on her knees, she fell before the blade. "Lysis-man, you, like me, had a cursed marriage. But I am not to blame. I cannot let you hurt my children anymore." The Lady grasped *Ferrus Eviscamir*. Her luminescent forearms gradually dimmed, though she was unaware that her aura was reacting with the sword. She rose to put Lysis, who remained on his back, atop the sarcophagus. Raising the blade over her erect spine, she struck to impale him through the torso. The sword passed easily through bone and chitin, then it slowed as it entered the marble beneath. So sharp was the blade, *Ferrus Eviscamir* sunk into the sarcophagus as if it were soft flesh. Sabina held tight to the hilt to ensure it was secure, but it resonated and pulses of pain shot through her hands forcing her to let go. She stumbled toward the exit.

Affixed to the stone, Lysis drowned in his past. The sword designed to heal the elder queen was now stuck through him, pinning him like a bug in a naturalist's cabinet. Was he just another specimen of the Doctor's now? No doubt, he had lost control over his mind. *Ferrus Eviscamir* was intent on eating his aura. Lysis used his sorcery to hold the sword's enchantment at bay.

Lacey climbed to the top of *Ferrus Eviscamir*'s hilt, her legs straddling it. The doll roosted atop the sword while staring down at her prey. Lysis saw only his son Erolen looking down at him, the youngest of his and Maeve's offspring. His boy's feet swayed as if he was suspended on a swing set. He had failed to protect the other ten offspring from dyscrasiac horrors, which weighed his soul heavily, but Erolen was special. The boy was the only one slain by his father's hand.

The sock-doll Bailey lingered nearby, under Lacey. With empty eye sockets, he stared at Lysis. Bailey remained at attention, awaiting orders.

Departing, Sabina held the fragmented threshold of the crypt for support. Her colony of wasps circled her as a frenzied whirlwind. "May you find peace imprisoned alone," she said, then turned away.

O N THE CHROMLECHON Theater's stage, Grave flaked away Echo's ossified skin. It sloughed off in thin, brittle shingles.

Even so, the boy lord still appeared as a stone sculpture. Dozens of children watched, hoping the Doctor could revive him so they could watch another performance. "Showtime is over, children. Our lords are both subdued. Let us go to another stage, the Pyre atop the Keep. It is our turn to perform for them. We have lots of work to do."

The golem lifted Echo's rigid body, and carried him atop the Chromlechon's crest. He placed the Gray Foundling before the Pyre. The children welcomed the Pyre's warmth in the wind-worn courtyard. Sitting in a circle, Cecelia and the other drained girls were regaining color. The fire pit's perimeter was now lined with cressets and braziers. A bonfire on a bed of white coals safely burned in the center. Smoke infused their skin with vibrancy. They worried for Echo. He looked like a limestone statue. They did not associate the boy lord with a threat. Last they had seen him, he was performing on stage. Now he was completely still. It seemed that Echo suffered from some mysterious illness.

"Fear not, children. Lord Echo will recover. He needs help, as does Lord Lysis. We all have nightmares—and hopes. I need you to draw yours. Or sculpt them. Transmit them to substance anyway you can. You do not need to present your art to me for approval. Merely recreate them, then put them in the fire. Your fears will be consumed, and hopes given chance. You will feel relieved. Your art will feed the fire. It will heal you as it strengthens the lords. Commence."

The Doctor distributed ink, paints, and quills. Most children obeyed by decorating fabric and parchment. Some rolled their sheets into tubular snakes without drawing on them. One boy manufactured dozens by himself. He seemed to enjoy the sparks issued each time he contributed to the fire. His juvenile laughter was contagious, melting away others' anxiety. Gloom evanesced. Hundreds of paper sprites danced in the variegated flames. These writhed as they celebrated life atop the cinders. The works had a symbiotic connection with the fire. They were not incinerated as the children expected. Instead, the papers' edges kindled as the art and fire exchanged energies.

Several children were too unsure or confused to participate. Indeed, Helen and Sharon remained at Echo's feet. Sharon could not be lured away. She clung to his ankles as if he were Lacey. In turn, Helen hugged her friend. The two had hardly uttered a word since arriving.

The Doctor attempted to reverse their descending spiral. He inspected the white-haired girl who was draped with a cougar hide. Helen did not match eyes with the golem, choosing to stare into the flames. However, her spiritual guardian did. In fact, Angie did not break her stare as she lay on her host's shoulders. Helen's innate creativeness was blinding. Her aura emanated from her like a heat wave, rippling the surrounding ether.

Grave said, "Listen now. Draw your guardian angel. Doing so will help bring your memories back. Making art heals. The lords need healing. You do too."

Reluctantly, Helen accepted some paper and drawing utensils. She did not know what Grave was talking about, nor was she in the mood to draw. She instead balled up the sheet. After unwrapping it, she examined the folds as if reading her palm for secrets. She cast more readings by repeating the process. Her scrying sheet eventually lost all its wrinkles as it became smooth, pliable, and indecipherable. Did this mean her future was bleak? Impulsively, she stuffed it in her mouth. She had been hungry, and angry, but eating paper proved impossible. She gagged, spit it out. She offered it to her pelt's mouth. Angie refused to bite. Helen rolled the parchment into an egg shape and tossed it into the Pyre.

Embers sparkled and took flight as the offering landed with the other animated sprites. Helen watched in awe as her contribution refolded itself. In moments, it assumed a blended shape of the feline sprite, the one that had led them to the mountain, with that of Angie's character. The pelt remained on Helen's shoulders of course, but she was compelled to pet it to confirm.

Doctor Grave could *see* with his undead vision what Helen could only vaguely sense. Through Helen's creativity, her emotions had been transferred into the paper cat. Angie's spirit had metastasized. Synergistically interacting with the fire, taking in Lysis's soul fire, the protective lioness of her memory was reborn. Brilliant white *lapis elixir* glowed in her arteries. The feline guardian spirit flared. It swaggered out of the Pyre leading a legion of other sprites of the same physical size. As it exited the ring of cressets, two wings opened on its back to billow in the wind.

Doctor Grave knelt before this parade. *"Your sprites serve a fallen lord, held captive by his past and a colony of diseased. You have risen from his ashes. He is Lord Endenken Lysis and his past consumes him. Go to him. Head north, "* Grave pointed. *"You will sense his location since the* lapis elixir, *his white ichor, burns within you as it does me. We are his minions. Take yourselves, his blood, to him. Fuel him. Free him of the memories that ail him. "*

Immediately the procession took flight, swirling in a spiral ever upward, creating a thunderous whirlwind. Arcs of lightning flashed. Fireflies sailed the pulsing cloud: first green, then tangerine, then brilliant lunar gold, then scarlet, then pearly white. All the children awed at the spectacle of fireworks which they had helped give birth to. Yet the wind was harsh, so they held each other's hands and huddled.

The cyclonic tempest gusted north. At the storm front was an enflamed cat effigy, the leading clouds of which assumed its emerald tinge and Angie's face. The Pyre flock sailed the sky with saintly haste. Racing over the land it rushed through the sunken district of Qual. Hence the clanhold which was already coated in volcanic powder suffered yet another ghostly storm. The tempest swelled every mile it traveled, accelerating until it crashed headlong upon the parade of Sabina's dolls before the chateau.

L ADY SABINA WALKED awkwardly, her legs still unwilling to change from their saddled position. Her parasol functioned as a crutch, aiding her traverse of the ruined basement. After countless years, she clambered out of her tomb.

"Now. I am free. I...," she panted, "... have returned."

She basked in the vibrancy of the manor house. Commotion filled the Hall of Mirrors. It was often intense, either full with people resonating with energy or, conversely, completely empty and eerily silent. In either case, it always displayed beautiful dresses on people or manikins. Presently, the Hall was packed. Was this masquerade in her honor?

Parasol spinning over her shoulder, she joined the ranks of concentric streaming rows of celebrants donning bustled dresses, beside bouncing dancers with frilled collars, all reverberating with the humming din of a stringed quartet. Yet she was weak and had not danced in decades. In seconds, she tripped over her own feet and fell as if she was a pathetic drunkard. Embarrassed, she attempted to rebound. But her torso ached. Larvae spewed from her open womb. She collected these, then slowly stood.

Strangely, no one came to her aid. The celebration continued unabated.

Sabina surveyed the Hall. Apart from the celebrators, a little girl with dark hair scurried around the adults. Girls were not usually welcome at parties, though she, as part of the regal bloodline, had been allowed to attend. Stealthily sneaking around, the girl ensured no one was looking, save Sabina, and then slipped off a glove from a manikin to try it on. Sabina recalled behaving like that. Then she looked in the mirror and saw her true younger self. It was as if her memories had been captured by the mirrors, and now were replayed. That girl was her.

"Lord? Lady? Do you see that girl?" Sabina asked a couple who were sipping wine. They rudely carried on their conversations, sustaining their laughter and smiles. More revelers passed, and eventually Sabina decided to reach out to stop a passerby. "Lord? Excuse me." She touched them, or what should have been them, but their bodies were intangible. Were these illusions? She touched the dress on the manikin that her past-self had touched. It was still solid. How can it be that historic shadows appear more real than the corporeal realm?

The sun did not shine through the windows. The exterior was blocked with gray stone. Apparitions illuminated this place with their eternally burning coronas. Ghosts walked beside her. She attempted talking to a few more, but none acknowledged her presence—let alone recognized her. The past blended with the bleak present.

Childish singing suddenly pervaded the chamber. Six dolls holding hands waltzed to her side, their eyes brilliant, glowing blue. Their stitched mouths sang spectral tunes:

"Now mother has arisen, she'll mother us again,
And you'll know, and we'll say so.
She'll raise us children with tighter rein,
O, poor old Lord!"

Sabina cradled her opened womb-hive as they ushered her out of the Hall of Mirrors and up to exit the manse. She climbed marble stairs leaning on her parasol. The celebrations faded as she left. Outside she saw her colony of minions and that which they possessed. Sabina also saw the ruined land. She recalled a blizzard she had seen as a child that coated all in deep snow, as if a huge, icy tapestry had been unfurled to smooth out the geography. Everything was buried. Her past included.

Her children rejoiced at her presence.

"Look at what I can do, Ma," a puppet yelled while riding the once-Queen's abdomen, the eldritch mount's six legs tethered to as many rows of puppets tugging on ropes. Her master, the Gray Lord Lysis, remained incapacitated in the crypt. The minions had essentially neutralized the once-Queen. She was not panicking, nor was she content. The shafts and wagon rigging encumbered her movement; its bed proved an adequate stage for acrobatic dolls.

Sabina's memories did not match reality. She had awakened in a hell in which ghosts were colored and the tangible was not. Hundreds danced atop her buried city. Discordant cries of attention-seekers penetrated her maternal soul:

> *"... mother has arisen, she'll mother us again,*
> *And you'll know, and we'll say so..."*

Lady Sabina raised her decorative umbrella. From under, she cackled maddening. Drops of rain drummed the parasol. White blood condensed to sprinkle the land. Stray drops struck her exposed hands. Each stung. Where they collided on her skin, hoarfrost grew. Sizzling reactions occurred between her blood and Lysis's ichor. Crystalline bruises smoked.

She dared to look up at the rain clouds.

A frosty vortex careened about the manor. Flocks of opal-veined paper-sprites raced in spirals. It was full of childish nightmare shapes: prismatic effigies of orphaned children seeking lost toys, fears of spiders' antennae groping about, and wailing parents. Sabina examined these juvenile haunts. The aerial tide crashed over the submerged city of Qual. Waves of aerosolized *lapis elixir* lapped against rooftops.

A butterfly-like invitation floated about the Lady. The storm seemed to have delivered a personal message. *This note reeks of Lysis blood.* She motioned to swat it, but the sprite fluttered away on its own. It did not come looking for Sabina, necessarily. It, like the storm, sought Lord Lysis and his quarry of stolen dolls.

The chromatic sprites descended on the dolls. A numinous battle erupted between minions of undead gods over children's toys. Sock puppets tugged at their own limbs, and those of others, and sprites crawled upon them, plucking at the wasps that infested their stuffing. The rope bearers released the once-Queen from her tethers so that they could defend themselves.

Angie's avatar surged out of the whirlwind's currents. It found firm footing on the ground, green sparks flaring with each step as it charged toward the manor house. Smokey, Shadow, and Queen-Bee sprang out of prowling to follow. Helen's cat family had reformed. Their fiery souls amplified as they pounced forth in confident strides.

In the crypt below, four Barbers of stone stood as sentinels, utterly still and obedient. The immobilized Endenken Lysis lay before them impaled on his own enchanted sword. The undead, piebald Spotty lounged in a curl around a statue's shoulder. Lacey, whom Lysis confused for Erolen, still swung her feet atop *Ferrus Eviscamir's* hilt. Bailey watched from behind the blade.

"Erolen, watch out!" Lysis yelled from upon his back. The cats flooded the chamber. Opalescent ether splashed under their feet, frothed about the chamber, and eddied. The ghostly boy dropped from his roost into the roiling magic.

The cats stretched on their hind legs while clawing at their undead sister. Spotty was surrounded by Shadow and Smokey. Crazed meowling, hissing, and howling pervaded the crypt. Bailey targeted Queen-Bee, grappling her stomach. She tucked, rolled, and scratched. In seconds, Bailey was reduced to four sundered socks. Buckwheat hulls and larvae emptied fast. Queen-Bee joined the fray against Spotty. The diseased cat lashed out, lacerating its mother. The tabby fell as her offspring fought. Blue blood ossified when contacting red. The living cats were no match for the undead feline.

Meanwhile, Erolen stumbled toward the incarnation of Angie. The fiery sprite launched toward the doll, knocking it upon its back, paws on shoulders. It then devoured the doll's aura, consuming all traces of Lysis's boy. Erolen's likeness vanished. He transformed into a worn, leather doll. Angie then burrowed into the doll's stuffing and picked out the wasps. White and blue mixed. Lysis's *lapis elixir* fueling the sprite, already a stable form of liquid stone, maintained its state. However, the diseased cyan blood which it contacted sizzled, becoming gray and hard, until the insects ossified. Soon, Lacey was just an inanimate doll again while the infesting wasps petrified.

Paper-Angie, whose brilliant corona faded to lime-green

as it catalyzed reactions, sprung atop Lysis. Her fire licked his face. Navigating the blade in his chest, she nibbled at visages of his family. Her priming canceled his memories. Maeve's effigy vanished. Yet the sprite was a temporary form, and the more she consumed the more she waned in power. Angie's edges burnt. She disintegrated, her green entity was sucked into *Ferrus Eviscamir*.

The room cleared of nightmares as the battle subsided. The ghost of Erolen no longer hovered above Lysis. Not immediately aware that he was skewered, he gazed at the hilt wondering why it was positioned so awkwardly. The room felt empty, as if he had been watched by someone, a woman, who was just here a moment ago… his wife! He looked around while struggling to remember her name, which would not come. He grew irritated as the sword limited his movement. Regaining his own volition, Lysis grabbed the hilt and pushed it away from the stone. He stood renewed.

Three carcasses lay at the base of the Barbers. Once-Spotty had killed its own family. It sprang toward the risen lord. He responded.

Ferrus Eviscamir cut through Spotty's spine.

Lysis used the blade to harvest the astral signatures of the cats and dolls which belonged to Sharon and Helen. Then he gathered the physical toys to return. Lysis first collected Bailey, knotting his limbs to his trunk. Lastly, the skeletal lord picked up Lacey and left with a clear mind.

LYSIS STRODE FROM the manor house's third floor, via the bay windows. Atop powdery dunes, he approached the kneeling, mad Sabina.

As much as the past haunted Lysis, the present haunted Sabina even more.

Lysis laid *Ferrus Eviscamir's* blade on the parasol's canopy. It stopped twirling. Shifting the weapon aside with a flick, the umbrella launched from her frail grip. Sabina was exposed. She attempted to stand. She faltered and fell onto her side. Larvae spilled from her belly. These effervesced in the puddle of white ichor pooling about her. Cerulean insects turned to stone, soaked in magical blood.

Ichor did not react like other blood. The lord's own had changed over his life and afterlife: from the Muse-infused red, to dyscrasiac-blue, to eucrasiac-white. He had obtained power that he failed to understand. He maintained a telegraphic relationship with this colorless rain which was his blood. It belonged to him. Was it *him*? Was each drop a distant extension, as is every drone of an insect colony? Did he have a *colony*? As rain came down, he saw visages of himself staring back from the careening drops. His essence splashed upon the beaten mother, cleansed her of the will to fight. Each aliquot froze the skin on contact, assuming ghastly shapes with human appendages.

"My children!" Sabina cried. Creamy raindrops ran down her cheeks in rivulets. They froze into sentient hoarfrost.

Lysis towered over her. "You have no children, my Lady. You had stillborn when alive, and a colony of insects past death.

Your offspring are not human. You have your husband Derryk to thank for that. Your time has passed. Your clan is gone."

She read his soul. "You? You have killed your own family?"

He tried to remember his own past. It was incomprehensible, save for fragments of betrayal. His memories had been shorn from his mind. Only obtuse scars remained. "I kill the corrupt. Family or otherwise, it matters not."

"You were a father, though. A father! How could you?" Sabina asked. "Were any of you Lysis Clan decent?"

"I see your soul as you see mine. You would have been a good mother. Yet illness strikes the good as well as the indecent." He reached toward her chest. He transmuted her sight, birthing illusions of willow branches to weave through the air—through her.

Sabina *saw* these tendrils as Derryk's branches, snaking like filamentous worms, threading their way into her ribcage. She muttered her last words under her own volition, "I know what you are. Womb-ripper…"

Lysis then possessed the heart of Sabina with his blood, displacing her dyscrasiac blood with his *lapis elixir*. Her wasps instantly faded. The parade of dolls ceased motion and singing. Her minions lost their animation.

Lady Sabina rose under his control. She remained standing as Lord Lysis tore out the hive, extinguished the womb. Larval pips spilled out and shattered into powdery puffs.

The Lord compelled Sabina through her manse to the Hall of Mirrors. She had no way to resist. He stripped the

manikin wearing the dress she had always fancied as a child;
he replaced the Lady's ruined attire with it. Clothed again, she
concealed her injured womb. She climbed the fountain and took
a seat on the vacated plinth. She accepted the umbrella from
Lysis, and placed it on her shoulder. As such she was locked
into position, as the Barbers were, as the Lord transmuted her
flesh into stone. She joined her dead clan as a centerpiece in a
gallery of beautiful manikins.

Lysis had no intention of bringing any corpses back
to the Keep. He gathered the petrified Lady Nadeen and Lord
Donquason from the wagon outside. Sharon's parents were
positioned as the last rulers of the clan, leading a dance, their
injuries upon death masked in stone. Helen's parents became
pirouetting visitors.

The Lord freed the cocooned children from the basement. The living were allowed to disperse. All the raised children of Qual, the dead ones that had been possessed by Sabina,
were gathered. Lysis posed them around the fountain. Sabina
would mother again in still-life.

Completed with the memorial, he acknowledged Sabina
with a nod and bow. In her aura, he discerned effigies of a
woman with black curls. This Lady Sabina reminded him of
someone. Another woman. One whom he once loved.

"*You are free from the past, again. Congratulations,
Lord.*" Doctor Grave hailed via telepathy. "*A request, Lord.
Bring back some of Qualenson's bolts of fabric. We'll use those
to enhance the Pyre rituals.*"

"*I'll return with a wagonload of dolls. If I decide to*

keep you as a servant, you can return here later to gather what you may," Lysis huffed. *"Grave, I hope to see your devotion is clear from the upkeep of the Chromlechon. I expect to see Lord Echo."* The once-Queen strode closer on command. Then the wagon was hastily loaded with dolls, and he returned. Several dozen orphans followed at a healthy distance.

VII: Goddess's Womb

L ORD LYSIS APPROACHED his Keep from the Gorgepath. Prior to his adventure into Qual, the banks on either end of the causeway were relatively flat. Now corpses lay in heaps along the bog. Doctor Grave had removed the Ill Age charnel debris from the Chromlechon. A grotesque dike now contained petrified elders, human bodies, and inanimate manikins. To have moved so much mass in so little time, the golem must have employed sorcery. Skeletal remains stretched from the mounds like stubborn saplings in a haunted forest. The terrain that Lysis navigated reminded him of the abandoned apple orchards from his ancestral home, Gravenstyne Fortress, lying unattended like SanGules's manor house. The Lysis clan had no known living heirs or surviving estates.

Flies buzzed in clouds around Lysis's trailing wagon even as night bowed to day. The dawning sun splashed its light against the western slope of the Chromlechon.

A dozen colossal ants skittered about. Six-legged, undead

elders lumbered down the mountain, encumbered with loads on their elephantine tusks. These reanimated ants were missing legs and lacking antenna, wearing their history. Many deposited stone harpies, empty exoskeletons, and ossified humans. What did Grave do? Did he resurrect her colony? Why was Lysis not aware of their animation? *My blood is so dispersed, I know not where it is, or what it controls.*

The skeletal lord brooded atop the once-Queen as she sauntered. Insect drones ready to return to the Keep followed Lysis—or did they follow the once-Queen? Lysis dismounted, his feet sinking into the wet earth. He neared the bogs of black liquor. The Gray Lord addressed the nearest elder. It stood waiting. Lysis raised *Ferrus Eviscamir* between its antennae. It did not falter. Then he reached out mentally via the ether to test his blood's location and power. He felt the presence of eldritch larvae within the insect's shell. He commanded the larvalwyrmen to exit it. Multiple, entangled wyrms wiggled from seams in the chitin armor. Then the exoskeleton collapsed.

Lord Lysis stared at the larvalwyrmen. *Are these mine? Or do they answer to Grave?* They began to worm their way into the soil, seeking the melancholy of the bogs to wet their hide. Ever since Lysis and Echo emerged from the once-Queen's womb, the Underworld Forge, he had gained a connection with these fell creatures. He focused on one. Seized its white blood via sorcery. It ceased its animation. He picked up the hollow carcass and threw it onto the heap. *I remain in control.*

Lord Lysis remounted the conquered elder queen. Westward he marched, toward the Keep. The mounds around him undulated. Strange vapors lifted as sunlight warmed the moist mass. The piles had yet to settle. Suddenly his senses electrified. Drawing *Ferrus Eviscamir,* he locked onto the source of the disturbance. An eldritch soldier ant burrowed with its tusks a hundred yards away. It appeared as if it was digging or was being pulled under. Emerging with haste, its tusks had pierced a colossal centipede whose anterior was capped with a human torso. Sunlight blinded the writhing mutant as cyan spilled from its punctures. There was no need for Lysis to act. His minion had isolated the threat. A minute later, the petrified effigy of the hybrid lay with hundreds of other monstrosities.

Dyscrasia persisted.

The Blood Bogs rippled as the lord returned across the causeway, the larvalwyrmen writhing just under the surface to welcome him. Several emerged vertically, like limbless trunks, halting in air to salute their master. The once-Queen clambered up the outside of the Chromlechon, her wagon filled with toys and the promise of hope. The Keep was cleaner now. Gone were the rats, corpses, and debris. Children were wrapped in thin bed rolls around the Pyre, while several stirred and wandered un-supervised. Petrified Echo stood dormant near the Pyre. Lysis dismounted. *"Grave, where are you?"*

"I am in the Chromlechon, Lord."

"Get up to the surface."

Grave immediately tapped Lysis on the back shoulder.

"Doctor, do not use telepathy if you stand beside me." Lysis glared at the golem. A beautiful woman stared back from Grave's aura. It was Maeve's effigy. She was not alone. At her feet were effigies of the burning once-Queen. The emotions culled from the aura by Lysis had rejuvenated. "I see, Grave, that you have recalled your love for my steed."

"… and of Maeve, Lord. The memories regenerated naturally. Do not worry. I assure you from experience that yours will grow back too."

"You commanded the sprites to harm my soul."

"To cleanse it, Lord. I see your suspicion. Note, my actions speak of my loyalty. Had I not done so, you would still be in Qual, incapacitated like our fellow Lord Foundling has become." They walked toward the statuesque Echo.

Ferrus Eviscamir raised to Grave's neck, just below his mask.

"My Lord, understand that Echo molts. He is maturing. That is all."

Maintaining his blade on the doctor, Lysis examined Echo's soul. Then he looked about the courtyard to see the afflicted children. Cecelia's pallor had not recovered fully, her hair now graced with two gray streaks. Lysis kept his blade raised, as the Doctor stammered. "There was almost a tragedy. Echo had accidentally fed on his friends… he had just begun to pupate. The Foundling is dormant now within the casing of his own skin. He will emerge… with some assistance…"

"Has your assistance enabled him to become petrified?"

"Lord, the stone is just a shell. You can see that he lives, yes?"

Lysis paused. *Ferrus Eviscamir* pressed slightly deeper into earthen flesh.

Grave felt it in his best interest to explain more. "He inadvertently hurt the ones he adores."

"So have you and I."

"We control sorcery instinctively. He does not."

Lysis glared with skepticism. "He fears his power, Doctor. As he should. As *you* should. There is much about dyscrasia that bothers me, Doctor."

"Me too. The disease diminishes but persists." Grave assessed.

Ferrus Eviscamir lowered. "The Keep appears better now without the corrupted bodies."

Grave nodded to accept what approximated appreciation. "We are learning the ways of eucrasiac alchemy, as demonstrated with our Pyre's success. As your power rises, that stricken with dyscrasia declines."

"Doctor, I went on a quest to help the children, but in the end, they saved me. They empowered me through that Pyre. Such work better not have hurt them."

"On the contrary, it aided them, Lord. The mere act of having a purpose lifted their mental state. Some consider themselves nurses more than artists. Eventually, Echo will need special attention. Perhaps we can assign a child to him."

Dozens of Keepers wearing linen shifts clustered in a semicircle. Presently, a score more of the children that had followed Lysis from Qual gathered from outside. The contents of the wagon had lured them all. However, the skeletal warrior and the tusked ant he had ridden kept them at bay. Excited to join humanity, they shuffled closer.

"You resemble the horrors they encountered," Grave said.

"You must enjoy reminding me of that. I seek not their love, just their freedom." Lysis disconnected the once-Queen's harness. She scurried down a hole into the heart of the Chromlechon. Likewise, the lord walked away from the wagon. The children rushed in. The Keepers welcomed the outsiders.

Lysis took some delight in seeing several youths waken in the sunlight. They stretched their arms, yawning.

The Doctor judged the masses. "I may need to help them for a moment. Perhaps you could assist me from afar, my Lord."

Grave approached the wagon while Lysis kept his distance, scanning auras and signaling which children should be paired with possessions. The candy-striped Cecelia regained her knotted sock doll first, and she soaked it with joyful tears. A giggling crowd surrounded her as she celebrated. With Bailey tucked under her left arm and an extinguished brand in her right, she conducted the dispersing of dolls. Girls began sewing the limbless toys, renewing appendages when possible. Boys played immediately, whether dolls were whole or not.

"Doctor, Cecelia has it under control now. You need to help me. I have two more things in my personal custody. I must return Lacey and the soul of Spotty."

"You seek Helen and Sharon, Lord? They rest in the Theater. We shall go there shortly." The Doctor pondered before Echo's statue and the magical bonfire. "The Pyre does not heal him as much as I had hoped. I expected that the fire would soften his shell more."

"You intend to take him to the Gallwomb." Lysis deduced from the Doctor's thoughts.

"Yes, I suspect the Foundling needs the residual powers of his birthplace. Else he may not break free." The golem heaved Echo onto his shoulder. "Larvalwyrmen will suffice for efficient travel. There is a subterranean passage to the Gallwomb. The Theater is along the way." Many tunnels dug by the once-Queen's colony were flooded with oil. The melancholic liquor was pervasive, infiltrating fissures in the earth and the lower strata of the Chromlechon. "I have permission I presume."

Lysis glowered.

"Do you not trust me, Lord?"

"I trust nothing."

"Aye, Lord. Let us go the Theater now."

They arrived in short order. Helen and Sharon huddled behind the rearmost pews, the same place they had been hiding when Echo had had his episode. All children adopted secure places to hide. This was their spot. Grave placed the gray boy on the stage, then retrieved the girls. Helen and Sharon shuffled their feet following the Doctor. They did not see the skeletal lord in the shadows, his sword drawn.

Lysis stood behind the despondent girls. He raised *Ferrus Eviscamir* above their heads. Slowly he lowered it such that its astral flames mingled with their coronas. Memories spilled over them: Sharon's parents visiting Helen's home, buying furs, and the two chasing one another in the fields.

The spirits of Helen's entire clowder—Spotty,

Queen-Bee, Shadow, Smokey—all sprang from blade to pelt. Energy poured into Angie's hide, which swelled as would a sponge. Helen was then scarfed with the agglomerate, feline phantasm; her spirit was infused with power. Her parents' love streamed into her, too, inflating her self-esteem. She imagined her pelt stretching its hind legs straight out while yawning to expel sleepy spirits. Both Helen and Angie awakened.

Sharon would not remember how Lacey landed in her hands. Yet in moments she would realize that her doll had been returned. So refreshed, the survivor from Qual negated any worry of wasps, or wraiths, or lonesome travels. Lacey had been taken by demonic things, and only an angelic force could have brought it back.

Their eyes dilated as memories and dreams restored their souls. Sharon's last remembrance of her Papa transformed from a burned, infested corpse into a healthy, wigged royal. Her doting Mum regained her full influence again in her mind. Sharon heard echoes of her wisdom, and commands, while she hugged Lacey with gusto. Likewise, Helen squeezed Angie; in her mind, a litter of kittens rubbed against her while her father's bodiless voice encouraged her to adventure.

"Lord, they think of their parents, not you. You may want to hide. Your appearance may offset the healing."

Rising slowly, the girls scanned the Theater for the presence of supernatural guardians.

"Greetings," Grave welcomed them.

Their hypnotic melancholy dissipated faster and faster. Awakened from depression, their ears accepted conversation.

Helen and Sharon smiled.

Lysis remained shrouded from sight. He admired the children's auras. Helen's creative soul had saved him. He could tell that both were afraid of wraiths still. There was no need to show himself to scare them. Best leave. He had to govern the others now. *"Doctor, I go,"* Lysis said as he departed into shadow.

Grave replied, *"No worries, Lord. They do not need you presently. I will assign them tasks before I attend to Echo. Expect me within a few days."* He turned his attention to the girls. Grave feigned ignorance of Helen's name. "Who are you?"

Her front hands stretched awake, extended like lioness claws, lifted with Angie's pride. She mewed, "Helen."

"And you?"

Sharon straightened to attention, holding Lacey at her waist. "Sharon, my Lord."

Grave's leather mask muffled his chuckle. "I am not a lord. My title is 'Doctor.'"

Empowered with her doll, Sharon touched Echo. "He is cold. Is he dead?"

"No. Lord Echo is frozen."

Sharon grew excited, *"He's a Lord?"*

"Will he ever melt?" Helen asked, leaning in.

"His ichor is a liquid stone that resists freezing. Only his outer skin has hardened. But he will shed it."

The girls remained confused.

"Think of it this way. You children lose teeth as you

mature. He loses all his skin. My next task, as doctor, is to get him out of that shell when the time is right. I will need to take him away. In my absence, you can help prepare his home." Sharon and Helen followed the doctor as he went to the store-rooms behind the Theater.

"This place reminds me of my Da's beamhouse, with all the cauldrons. Do you cook dinner in these?"

"Echo used to sleep in one of them. I wouldn't use these to cook in, not so near the Theater. These were for… for experiments…"

"But you've an herb garret here. Mmmm, this one smells nice. Oooh, is this dried lavender?"

Grave rummaged through his stores. "Yes, Helen, that keeps bugs away."

Sharon reminisced on her mother's perfumed soap. She placed a sprig in her hair. Then she located a broom and began obsessively sweeping. "Mum always said 'be clean.'"

Helen said, "Mine said 'go out to play.'"

"Playing will only get you dirty." Sharon swept.

"Like you? I'm not the one soiling my dress," Helen teased.

"I *am* clean." Sharon inspected her clothes despite her disbelief. It was difficult to know when Helen saw reality. "You could help tidy up."

"Hmm, I wonder what the Doctor says I should do."

"Well, Helen and Sharon," Grave replied, "you are charged with a great responsibility. You must help us restore humanity. We will begin training immediately. There are many rules to learn."

"I have sweeping to do. Then this storeroom needs organizing. Dusted, too."

"Humanity does need housekeeping. In time, I have other plans for you, Sharon. For now, I dare not interfere." Grave paused to read Helen. "I do need an adventurer to retrieve Echo's dolls."

"Where are they?"

"Echo dropped them down that hole in the floor when he pupated."

Helen asked, "He *what*?"

"When his skin hardened, he lost control over his puppets. They fell. An old nursery is down there. Find his dolls. They are named after Lady Aleece, Lordson Bryhan, and... one other. A bird of some sort. The Gray Foundling will desire them soon enough." He turned to go, confident that she would finish the challenge. The Doctor procured a hefty butcher blade, *Ferrus Hewnmaw,* from storage, then picked up Echo and left through the maze of corridors behind the Theater. The girls bid him *adieu.*

"That hole is really big." Helen gazed at the giant bones serving as struts across the pit. Helen was reminded of when her Mama dressed chickens, cutting off heads and emptying the ribcages. This hole looked a lot like the inside of a bird. "The bottom is missing."

"Mum would have said 'no' to this. Too dangerous."

"Sharon, come on. The Doctor says I need to go." Helen peered into the hole. "There are no real walls down there. Just rocky caves. Lots of shadows."

Sharon asked, "What do you expect to find in the dark when you explore? Why leave the safety of the hewn walls?"

"I don't need walls." Helen smiled. "The Doctor told me to go down there. Want to come?"

"I'm staying up here."

"Doctor said I have to go. Come on Angie, time to explore." Helen descended as a cougar, managing to hold a lantern as she crawled. The wall appeared to undulate like water as the light bobbed. She reached the bottom in minutes. It was only moments later when she called back. "Sharon?"

"Yes?"

"I see lots of crystal people here. Statues without heads. Ouch!" Suddenly the lantern light extinguished with the sounding of crashed glass.

Sharon dropped the broom and scrambled to the edge, "Helen?"

"I stepped on something sharp. Should be fine, except I can't see. Can you come down with another lantern?"

"I'm not going down there. Into that!" Sharon shouted.

"Really?"

"I'm holding another lantern closer. Is that helping?"

"No. You'll have to come down."

Sharon sighed, "I will get help. Don't get scared."

"I don't need help, actually." Helen called to the vacant Theater. "I just need light."

DOCTOR GRAVE DISMOUNTED the larvalwyrmen, still embracing Echo with his ax sheathed on his back. Ever comfortable navigating the Underworld, he arrived at a central island within the Gallwomb caldera. Grand shards of stone loomed all around. These were chthonic tors rent from the earth's surface. *Ferrus Eviscamir,* wielded by Lord Lysis, had done the cutting. Lysis had unleashed Cypria's litter. Ended her. Vestiges of the dead succubus smoldered from every crevice. Yellow, sulfurous clouds floated low. Fragments of egg shells lay scattered about, along with ossified, stillborn wraiths. Wielding the sister blade *Ferrus Hewnmaw* and one of Cypria's unique offspring, the Doctor walked forth.

The wyrm retracted into the subterranean lake, obeying commands to remain near the banks. The black oil bubbled, not due to heat, but from toxic gases emitted from geological reactions. Geysers plumed intermittently. The energies under the earth had yet to equilibrate.

Moonlight revealed the surrounding canyon only in places. The tortured landscape reached into the sky as much as it sank into the Underworld. Monolithic boulders protruded at odd angles from canyons submerged in shadow, each mountainous tip seemed to point toward a different constellation. Every uprooted slab appeared as a windswept tombstone threatening to teeter over. The exposed sides revealed colossal fossils forever encased in earth. Astral steam emitted from crevices between strata and bones to flow upon invisible currents.

Grave ventured inland where he had to rely on his

undead sight. He looked for a place flush with Cypria's aura. Although her blood had been tainted blue, her impregnation by insectan, human, and avian seed had turned her womb, her gargantuan infested gall, into a cauldron in which *lapis elixir* formed. Echo was only one manifestation hatched. Most in the litter were hybrid wraiths. The prismatic, opal aura of their eucrasiac energies lingered. The Doctor tracked bright, sparkling veins within the rock, following them as they flared brighter and brighter, until he found a brilliant artery.

This rich font of energy had attracted others. A cyan-bloodied Picti must have roamed here, then fell as its body reacted to the eucrasiac vapors. Then another came to feed on it. Poisoned, it also succumbed. This repeated, with scavenger following scavenger. Now awash in ghostly light, six gargoyles bent over the offerings coming before. The dyscrasiac mutants fed upon their own kind. Two eaters were naked, winged females. All were descendants of Clan Lysis, or afflicted by their blood. Without proper masters, such as the once-Queen, the diseased did not form large colonies. Indeed, it was strange to see so many together.

The Doctor placed Echo down, then raised *Ferrus Hewnmaw*. He waited patiently for the cannibals to finish. Their full bellies would only slow them down. Perhaps the white fire of the astral plane would consume them all and battle could be avoided. "The beasts here do not know the ways of alchemy, my Lord Echo. But look. They must detect my scent."

A dozen sparkling eyes shifted toward him. All glowed azure with ill blood. Three males were helmed with bleached, avian skulls and armored in exoskeletons. Their only weapons were lengthy talons.

The females took flight. Meanwhile, the male ghouls rushed on the ground en masse.

Grave extended his ax and waited. His apron was ready to be wetted. Grave turned the blade toward himself and sliced his left arm. White ichor poured through his earthen hide. He dropped *Ferrus Hewnmaw.* He clenched his fist repeatedly, magical blood pooled into his palm. This melee would begin empty-handed.

An instant before collision from the two aerial gargoyles, the larvalwyrmen snapped out of the black water, its length smashing one while the tip lashed the other. Breathless, the females struggled to regain footing. Blue ichor shot in spurts from the ripped wing of one. She curled up screaming. The other was temporarily dazed from its collision.

The runners closed. Grave waved his left hand, full of his own blood, parallel to the ground in a hasty flash. *Lapis elixir* shot in spurts from Grave's self-inflicted wound. It sprayed the faces of the closest three, turning eyeballs to stone and blinding them on contact. He ducked, retrieved *Ferrus Hewnmaw* with two hands, and then swept it, pulverizing the legs of the sightless. Without eyes or legs, they were no longer a threat.

Recovering from the earlier stunning blow, the remaining female gargoyle sprung forward and latched onto Grave's back. She clawed at his leather mask.

He leaned backwards and launched his weight toward the lake. The load was removed immediately. Grave stood and turned to see the larvalwyrmen spiral around the winged foe, drag it under.

The Doctor ensured all carcasses were fully dismembered.

He carried Echo into the depths of the fissure where the aura of the Land was strongest. Cypria's maternal magic remained, sublimating in dense clouds from the rocks. Echo's mutating body bathed in the location of his original birth. The lingering soul-fire of his dead, godly mother enflamed his aura.

"Here, Lord Echo, you will finish your transformation. Shed your skin. Hatch again."

The Doctor inspected the demigod lord. Echo's head was softening, especially around the eyes; without intervention, these might rupture prematurely and affect future vision. Conversely, the segments around his abdomen where too hard; this added undue strain on sections that needed to lengthen. Leaving Echo, Grave revisited the pile of ghoul pieces to collect an arm. The golem pressed his clay finger into the sundered limb, gathered some dyscrasiac gore, and used this to paint thin layers of blue over the Gray Foundling's eyes. A thin layer of stone crystallized upon the globes. Then he cleaned his fingers and held his left arm, which kept weeping ichor. To avoid contaminating any of his treatments, his wet right hand then worked the *lapis elixir* into the folds of Echo's abdomen, which accepted the liquid and softened.

It was time for Echo's body to work at its own rate. The Doctor stood at attention with ax in hand. All was quiet now as he stared at the surrounding canyon. All walls were marbleized with ichor veins. This ruined Gallwomb resembled the Doctor's own skin, his mineral flesh being infused with Lysis's blood.

"*Lapis elixir* is densely veined here." The golem Grave contemplated, "Lord Echo, your flesh may be more organic than mine, but we share ichor. Our blood is molten stone. This land is like us. It is living, pumping *lapis elixir*, and radiates the life force you require. Worry not, my Lord Foundling, you will emerge from this womb healthy again."

L YSIS SAT ATOP the once-Queen in the Pyre's flames, a demigod enflamed in his own ethereal blood. His eleven children's effigies formed a ring and goaded him:

> "*Four and twenty gray Lords*
> *Fail to save the world*
> *Ashes! Ashes!*
> *We all will burn!*"

The coals simmered below. Prismatic flames reached higher. A miniature effigy of Erolen crawled along his arm like a spider. Multiples of Erolen emerged all over his legs. Lysis brushed them away. The memories kept returning. Maeve haunted him next. Her dark hair snaked around him, wrapped about his arms, and merged with the creases in his chitin armor. Her voice struggled to coalesce, never becoming coherent. It remained a haunting whisper.

Lysis held onto to a hope that her spirit was still alive, knowing all vestiges of her had been absorbed into the vacuous oil in the bogs. He strained to interpret her voice. The effigies seemed to mouth a message for him: … *am… sorry*. Were those his words echoing in the gloom, or hers?

Vaporous simulacra of Maeve seeped out of Lysis's horns, then sank as a thick haze that interfered with his vision. He would have to look through her to see anything else.

"The past respawns like a cancer. I cannot erase it completely. Only diligence will contain it. Goodbye, Maeve. Again."

Endenken Lysis held out his arms for his sprites to perch. Scores of locust-like minions landed and nibbled on his corrupted spirit. He thought of his Picti ancestors, worshippers of the once-Queen, how he turned against them, started his own family outside his bloodline despite the dangers of disease, and how dyscrasia destroyed Maeve and the children anyway. The self-destructive nature of the Lysis clan lived on still. He could never divorce himself entirely from his origins. His haunting past had almost ended him in Quall. Endenken Lysis was the source of his own nightmares, so he had to rely on external forces to quell them. The Keeper's offerings, the animated sprites, provide this function symbiotically: as Lysis consumed the children's creative work, the sprites would extinguish his phantoms. "I am not a monster like you," he said to the once-Queen. The tusked colossus did not reply. "I do not consume human blood as you did. I merely eat emotions and feed on memories as others feed on mine."

SHARON ARRIVED IN the topmost courtyard, sheepishly looking for help. The Doctor was not present. She was too afraid to speak to Lord Lysis. Numerous children were on the outskirts of the fire with a bossy girl instructing them. Approaching, they offered Sharon paper, quills, and inks. Yet she was not looking to create.

"You, there. Sit with us. You shan't be wandering about as a lone wolf forever. You need to join us."

Sharon turned away. She was on a mission of her own. Distancing herself to the other side of the Pyre. Here she paused, twenty yards away from the mounted skeleton. Her heart pounded even though the Lord was passively resting. His skeletal appearance unnerved her. Nevertheless, she needed assistance.

The pigtailed one caught up to her. She had striped leggings which Sharon scrutinized as the looming voice showered down. The voice was familiar. "You want to communicate to him? You can't walk into the fire, silly. You'll get burned. Now start listening to me. Take this chalk and paper. He'll understand whatever you write on it."

Sharon reached for the tools. They dropped as she failed to grab them. Franticly, she got on her knees. The chalk had cracked. Why was this girl pressuring her?

"Stand up!" the taskmistress commanded, tapping the disobedient, kneeling girl with her bone torch.

Sharon kept her eyes low. She did not like conflict. This was not a good time. Helen needed her help.

"Are you Sharon of Qual?' Her tone nearly cracked with joy. It was Sharon... but then her heart sank. Sharon was too ill to understand, too distraught, to recognize Cecelia in return. If Sharon was here in the Keep, then her parents went the way of their clan. Grief still hung on her heavily.

Finally, she answered. "The same. Sharon, daughter of Regent Donquason. My father rests in heavenly fields now. As does my Mum." Sharon looked up now, focused on the girl's freckles. This one's orange hair had been bleached, like Helen's had in the Gallwraith's nest. A knotted sock puppet was held against the girl's side. "Bailey? Cecelia?"

Had dignified ladies of the court been allowed to hug, they would have. The two hastily curtseyed and exchanged kisses on either cheek. Then they inspected each other.

"Bailey is in sore need of darning!"

Cecelia reached to adjust Sharon's hair. "My dear, you still smell faintly of lavender. And your tooth is crooked."

Sharon laughed, ignoring the observations while celebrating. "Come, dearest Cece. My friend has gone below the Theater and is without light. I planned to get help from the Pyre. See, I drew a torch. Can you help? It seems you know how things work around here."

"The children need leading else they act like barbarians. Lord Lysis and Doctor Grave have too much to do to worry about details. But their magic can help us. Finish your art while I light my torch," Cecelia extended her brand in the Pyre and relit the tip.

Sharon drew, then fed, her fears into the Pyre. Lysis

watched. As Sharon's donation took form, he sent the minions from his arm to join her. Sharon giggled as the flock of the sprites fluttered about. Some were humanoid fairies with wings. Others hovered like hummingbirds. Many more were just tiny embers, no bigger than fireflies. All circled her head. Dazzling ribbons of light trailed each.

They ran off to the Theater, a cloud of lights spinning around them. Sharon yelled as they went, "Helen! Helen, I bring a friend. And lightning bugs!"

B LINDED IN DARKNESS, Helen wandered in the ossuary on her hands and knees. She investigated by touch. Her fingers delved into piles of spherical beads, connected strings of pearls, and frayed ribbons. She prowled atop a pile of polished artifacts and rounded shields. Did all this fall from the Theater above? It must have been a treasure room once, or a museum.

"Helen, I am back!" Sharon's voice resonated from the Theater above. "Are you well? Don't worry, I brought help."

Helen fondled the curios, in no hurry to leave. "Sharon, there are piles of treasure here. Wands. Armor. Coins. They must be beautiful. You should come down and join me. The items here need organizing."

Lights filtered down like dust from the heavens. Helen imagined she was hunkered in her home meadow again. It was midnight. The night sky was pitch black save for the falling stars. Her group of cats waited nearby. She bent lower, laying upon the trove, recalling the wondrous effect of firefly swarms.

The sprites descended slowly. Eventually they revealed the treasure: bones and body parts! The ribbons she had caressed were bundles of human hair; the wands were actually humerus bones boiled clean; the shields were chitin shells from colossal eldritch ants.

"Ahhh!" Helen back peddled thinking the relics were still living. She inspected the oddities by prodding them with a lengthy bone. Soon she realized all were dead, and then she calmed. She had always been interested in animal remains, having collected them for years. Never had she seen any relics like this. Some were crafted from glass. Others were warped and stretched, as if an artist had worked them in a furnace. Helen looked upon the refuse with renewed interest. She sifted with her hands through mounds of oversized, hollow centipedes.

Sharon asked, "Can you see the dolls that Doctor sent you after?"

Now she did. Helen scampered over to the where the burning sprites congregated. Two limp puppets lay. Her right hand grabbed the one-armed warrior. Her left hand took the feminine doll impaled with an iron needle. Both were sodden with cold liquid. Water, she presumed at first. She twirled around dancing with her lifeless partners. The smaller embers began to fade, so the room began to close about her. The sprites would not illuminate this place forever.

"Helen?"

Helen compressed the dolls as she danced. Now, glistening, pearlescent blood ran in rivulets down her forearms.

"Whoa!" If they bled, they might be alive. Helen dropped

the two dolls in terror. She stomped on them. The dolls made no attempt to respond. They were cold and dead as everything else was. Strange that they were soaked in white blood. They had fallen beside the third puppet to be reclaimed. Helen stared at the thing. It reminded her of the mutant Gallwraith from the fog. It was as tall as the other dolls, but inhuman. It looked like a chicken with extended legs and beak. Dead or not, she was not excited to touch it.

"Helen?"

Helen breathed deep, then collected the three figures. "Coming now." She clambered back toward the Theater but stopped in the chamber below as she encountered two girls. They looked like twins, one sporting a ponytail, the other pigtails. It looked like Sharon had found a cousin, a freckled one with striped socks.

Cecelia had seen the nursery before, and was less impressed than Sharon by the chamber's contents. Several corridors spilled into the ruined grounds. Glass baubles and bones lay in piles.

Sharon introduced the two.

"Found Echo's dolls," Helen showed Aleece, Bryhan, and the fowl-wraith. Sharon shied away from the avian figure and took the other two.

Celia stared oddly at the feral Helen, who displayed sprigs in her hair and was donned in fur. That girl was not from the civil world. Her eyes were overly glossy, penetrating beyond normal sight. Cecelia extended no kiss or curtsey. "Your friend is dirtier than you, Sharon. What *is* she wearing? We should clean her up. Discard the mangy pelt and we'll find you a shift."

Helen paraded about extending Angie's arms, the fowl clutched in her right hand. She stopped before Cecelia and blurted, "Nature painted you nicely. I had a spotted cat with a face like yours." Then she plopped back in the pile of bones while Cecelia massaged her cheeks contemplating her freckles. Helen meanwhile gathered a knotted mass of cartilage and bone which sparkled from its coating of glass shards. "See how beautiful these are? You two should wear these jewels."

Cecelia held her torch closer and grimaced. She knocked the offering away. The curios clinked like coins atop the refuse of chitin and crystal.

"She's from the outskirts, Cece. She sees things differently. Now come on, let's go up to the Theater where it's cleaner."

Sharon and Cecelia began their trek upward. Helen waited for time to demonstrate her independence. She played in a pile while the sprites from the Pyre floated about, encouraging her to stay longer. Eventually, she raced like an agile cougar to catch up to her peers, Echo's baby wraith in her clutches.

THE LARVALWYRMEN DEPOSITED Doctor Grave and Lord Echo on the banks of the Underworld cavern beneath the Chromlechon. It was so vast that, even with undead vision, neither could see the opposite shore. The glossy eldritch larva floated nearby, awaiting orders.

Grave said, "You are in no condition to journey on those new legs. They are longer than before. Rest here. Dry off. I have a surprise to show."

Lord Echo sat to watch the doctor wade into the melancholic sea, mount the wyrm again, then descend beneath the surface. Long minutes transpired. Echo remained too tired to move away. He could probably ascend without getting lost. Yet his transformation had drained him. His entire body ached. The best he could muster was stretching his legs and arms.

Keeping the Gray Foundling company were countless statues of harpies, men, and hybrid insects locked in eternal combat. The battle for the Underworld had been costly. In the Ill Age, civilians had been murdered for their blood to fuel arcane rituals. Many warriors also died in battle. The alchemical reaction between blue and red blood turned most into stone. Effigies of this war sat eerily quiet. Echo held onto a naive hope that the forms were still alive under their stone shells, containing latent existence under a thin casing that could be cracked free—like the one he recently shed. More likely, the diseased forms were completely solid now. Echo may also achieve such a state if he did not learn to molt without Grave's aid.

Eventually, bubbles broke the flat surface of the lake. A spear tip emerged rising like a flag staff. Oil canopied from its tip, stretching rather than dripping, until it finally pierced the viscous muck. The recoiling fluid radiated concentric ripples atop the black bath. Then Grave arose. A maimed body was draped over his shoulder. His left arm held several limbs and the spear shaft. Larvalwyrmen floated in the dark lake behind the encumbered doctor as he exited. On the shore, Doctor Grave sat the warrior's torso upright against stone. Then he deposited two legs and an arm. He laid the spear upon the corpse's lap. Oil had coated this exhumed, one-armed man. It seeped off him while the Doctor flicked globs of black goop from his apron.

"Bran?" Echo asked. Then he identified the phantom of Bryhan's mother on the spear. "Aleece."

"Yes. Your guardian is retrieved, Lord Echo," said Grave. "I'll teach you to reanimate him as you did your puppets. We will keep his body here until you heal enough. For now, we must keep going. Here, climb on my back."

"COME SHARON, IT is time to celebrate." Helen led her friend from the storeroom to the Theater stage. She carried a wooden tray with a lit beeswax candle and a decanter of water.

"What is the occasion?"

"The Doctor is bound to return with Echo any moment."

Sharon put her broom aside. She followed, with Lacey stuck in her apron pocket. "How do you know?"

"It has been two days. Lord Lysis has been visiting the Theater regularly."

"He's here? How do you know?"

Helen pointed toward the skeletal lord in the rear of the seating. "He is not pacing this time. And that sword of his is finally sheathed. He calms, so I guess he has good cause."

The girls sat on the Theater stage beside Echo's dolls.

Sharon attempted to braid Helen's hair, adjusting the silk ribbon that once belonged to Lacey. The beautification process was hindered. For one, Helen's hair was all entangled. Plus, the mane on her shoulders got in the way.

"Let us have a tea party. Make wishes again!"

Sharon replied, "The water is cold, and we have no tea cups." Lacey sat beside her.

"Nonsense." Helen curled her hands upward, joined. Her friend followed suit. They toasted.

"To serve a lord," Sharon sipped the air.

Helen closed her eyes. "To become a fairy."

Fʀᴏᴍ ᴀ ᴛᴜɴɴᴇʟ beyond the storeroom, Grave entered the Theater. Echo rode piggyback. The boy had metamorphosed. His arms remained human skinned, but were now bent like a mantis. Two small antennae quivered atop a bald brow. His lidless eyes seemed to swell out of their sockets.

"Doctor Grave, Echo is renewed and healthy."

"Yes, Lord. I am glad you see that." Grave and Lysis observed Helen's aura too. Her cat spirit remained intensely green and enflamed in the astral realm. *"Lord, we witness nascent power brimming in a new era. The Ill Age is over."*

Echo joined the girls. Sharon wetted a napkin from the decanter and began cleaning dirt off him. The Gray Foundling accepted this affection while he surveyed the Theater looking for something. Delighted to see the boy alert, Sharon asked

"What do you wish for, Lord Echo?"

"Angels. Puppets."

Sharon offered forth the dolls of Bran and Aleece. "He and his partner are right here." Helen presented the embryonic wraith. "And this thing too."

Echo took all three. He hugged them. "Puppets," he said.

"Doctor, the girls are not scared of Echo, like they are of me."

"True, Lord. But they need and respect you. In fact, the girls see you as a guardian angel, as do the children throughout the Keep. They need your protection. You are their daimon.*"*

Lysis inspected the ether on his body. His memories had been quelled. The more he *saw* what his past contained, and the more he witnessed the potential of the children being realized, he felt empowered. *"I think of them as my guardians."*

"I see." Echo spoke, maintaining his façade with the children. He had been eavesdropping.

"What do you see?" asked Grave.

Lysis said. *"We are* daimones.*"*

"Not children." The insectan boy stood up, reflecting on the dolls. Should he still have such toys? He contemplated the girls who held their own childish tokens. He sensed another youth watching from the shadows. It was one of the girls he had accidentally drained prior to his molting. Cecelia. She would not approach until he left.

Lord Lysis, *"You are still a child for now."*

Echo bent and, with crooked wrists and oddly articulated

arms, gathered his three toys. *"Angel Bran. Aleece. Sister,"* He embraced them and darted into the tunnels. The girls did not know where he went, but understood not to follow. Lysis and Grave knew that Echo ran to show the dolls to the exhumed warrior who shared the name Bran and whose body lay hidden in a recess in the lowest reaches under the Keep.

"When you are mature, Echo, you'll find security in weapons, not dolls," professed the Doctor to all telepathically.

Lysis did not disagree. *"Come, Doctor. We need to discuss the securing of this Keep. The children should not worry about wielding weapons."*

As the theater emptied of demigods, Cecelia skipped forward with her extinguished wand.

"Joining us for tea?" asked Helen.

Sharon smiled. "Cece! Please sit. Bailey can join ussss...," A burst of blood spurted from her lip as a tooth loosened. It did not fall out completely, remaining attached but bent out of position.

"Dear Sharon, you have no cups," Cecelia said. "Actually, you have no tea either."

Sharon shut her lips trying to assess the tooth. It resisted reinsertion.

"I saw you waiting. Are you afraid of Echo?" Helen interjected.

"I was a friend of Lord Echo." Cecelia flipped her bleached pigtails, as if that explained her decision. "I am now inclined to serve Lord Lysis and Doctor Grave. They control magic better."

"H'lp, plzzz," Sharon pleaded. She prodded her tooth with her tongue. "Can you pu' 't 'ack?"

Helen could not resist. She reached forward, grabbed, and pulled. The tooth came out instantly. Its departure was long past due.

"Eww. Gross," Cecelia turned her head.

"Wow!" Helen celebrated. She pored over the tooth. It was a polished jewel to her. And it was special, since her friend had grown it. A bead of red remained in the underside's cavity, but was otherwise polished like a pearl. "Can I keep it?"

Sharon giggled an assent. She did not desire the abject tooth, and was just relieved that the new one was remarkably grown already.

"You're mad!" yelled Cecelia.

"I am not angry at all." Helen refuted.

Cecelia sneered. "I meant that you are bizarre. You know. Crazy?"

As a rural urchin at heart, Helen was comfortable with being peculiar. She pawed the air and meowed partly because she enjoyed play, and partly because she enjoyed perturbing those who did not. Such interaction reinforced Helen's desire to be distanced from the others. Each day hence, the social order intensified. Sharon and Cecelia followed their innate desires to serve authority and provide order. The needs of the Lords were demanding.

Helen did not gain comfort with crowds. She preferred to take Angie exploring the ruins of the Keep. Whenever she got lost, fire sprites would eventually find her. There was little harm in adventuring inside the mountain. There was little harm in being alone.

O UTSIDE THE CHROMLECHON, threats endured, sparse though they were. Doctor Grave joined his Lord to survey the Land again. Lysis spoke, "There are still dangers out there. Do you see the gargoyles that crawl along the outskirts of the bog now? I see three."

"Yes, Lord. I see each. They are curious about the heaps of the dead. And they are hungry, but they fear your minions."

Lysis's insectan elders rearranged carcasses, spreading them out in regular intervals, standing them upright, draping limp bodies over poles, displaying Lysis's enemies from the Ill Age. He had them impaled alongside the anthropomorphic corpses. Not all were whole. Myriad heads were suspended on high, and truncated torsos were propped atop colossal bones. Here the dead were ornaments. Most were inanimate. Some were instilled with his *lapis elixir*. These would be his sentinels, ready to ambush any evil that infiltrated the Orchard.

"These dead grounds will appear as a forest soon. My Gray Orchard will form a barrier around the Blood Bogs. My minions will be sentries for the Keep."

"You have many." Grave prodded, "Are you reviving a colony?"

Lysis disregarded the remark. "This Gray Orchard will not be enough. The Chromlechon is too porous. We must seal the sides to fortify the Keep."

The Doctor pushed further. "Lord, the more minions you raise, the more creative energy you will require. You'll need a bigger Pyre. More children doing more sorcery."

"Train the children then." Lysis said.

"Aye, Lord. They will become your curators. They will heal your aura as you cast spells."

"We will need to guide Echo too."

Doctor Grave replied, "Echo is more hesitant than you Lord. He does not have the courage to practice his new arts."

"He is just a boy." Lysis walked away. "He grows."

Grave followed, "He is a Chromantis. I warn you. He can consume color, and may make the whole Land gray. The once-Queen feared such creatures."

"Nay, Doctor. He has a kind soul. Teach him to remain so. He need not become toxic. He needs to learn how to practice magic."

"Aye, Lord. I will have him animate something more than puppets."

Lord Lysis considered his own animation of those in his Orchard. "Start now, Doctor."

Grave departed.

GRAVE ENTERED THE stockroom behind the Theater, navigating a pile of empty jars to find Sharon sweeping the floor. He had left her organizing the stock of herbs, seeds, and oils about the garret. The Doctor had had the items arranged by their function first, then by their potency. However, in his absence, Sharon had removed the empty glasses and arranged the remaining alphabetically. He was impressed.

Sharon stood at attention. "Doctor, you are out of many herbs."

"My pantry has been raided to flavor meals. No worries, we have larger tasks to tackle. Wishes to fulfill." He walked closer. "Do you wish to serve the lord that the others fear?"

"Echo?" Her eyes dilated. The broom dropped. Her heart pattered. She had no idea of what she may be committing to if she agreed. What does it mean to serve a lord? What would her Mum say if she declined? Before she could apply any reason, instinct made her nod affirmatively.

Grave procured a blank leather canvas and ink bladders. These he gave her. She appreciated the quality of the hide. He acquired *Ferrus Hewnmaw* and a lantern as he began to leave.

"Follow me."

Sharon trailed for a time. The rugged terrain slowed her. "Doctor, I cannot keep up." Scared to leave the manicured corridors, she clutched Lacey to her waist.

"Jump on my shoulder. Trust me, I will carry you."

She weighed almost nothing compared to other things he had lifted. He carried her in the dark, down staircases, ramps, and vertical rock formations. She pressed her face against the Doctor's leather mask. It smelled of smoke. Eventually, she heard splashes but could not see the source. Outside her sight, the bogs in the underworld cavern undulated. It sounded as if an entire ocean surrounded them. The swimming of larvalwyrmen sounded like that of fish. She could not see Echo either, who was cuddled with dolls beside an oil-sodden, crippled warrior.

Shadows seemed to tug on her ponytail. Mysterious drafts pulsed on her exposed skin.

Grave said, "Without the Red Muse of the once-Queen burning, the larvalwyrmen are unable to develop and can't evolve as you do, Echo. Every year you will molt and emerge anew. The magic in your blood will no doubt evolve as powerful as Lysis's has. He has hundreds of minions in his possession. He will need as many curators to sustain him with creative powers. Now Echo, it is time for you to mature. You need to control more than mere puppets. And you will need at least one caretaker."

Grave handed the lantern to Sharon. The dim light now hovered mere feet above the ground, below many of the rock formations. Stalactites hung from utter darkness.

"Curator Sharon?" Echo said.

She curtsied. "My Lord, at your service."

"*No more hurt.*" Echo said to Grave, backing away. "*Not her.*"

"*Lord, you do not have to hurt her.*"

"*I have hurt.*"

"*Others you have hurt, true. We will limit your proximity to the others... you can remain reclusive. But we will train you to be controlled. We start today. Once you learn, you will only hurt those you want to.*"

They both observed the specimen, Lordson Bryhan.

Only Doctor Grave knew the difficulties of retrieving the body from beside the Underworld Forge. Such a feat would have been impossible for anyone else, even for one who could read signatures of souls adhering to bone. Yet the Doctor knew where the body was slain. Echo remembered the soldier having lost one arm, but did not recall the man being truncated of limbs. Grave remembered, though. In his new role under the Gray Lords, he was compelled to retrieve as many appendages as originally belonged to the body. The Doctor had already reattached the right arm and both legs. The body was still inanimate, sitting in a pool of melancholic oil, legs submerged, with his back slumped against stone. Warm light scintillated off his lamellar scale armor.

"How do we wake him?" Echo asked aloud.

Grave decided to speak out loud too, so that Sharon could learn a bit of the sorcery she had to nurse. "Lord, you must provide your blood to his heart. Once it pumps your ichor, then you will control his body and mind."

Echo did not respond nor move.

"What is the matter, Lord Echo?"

"I cannot do this."

"I will help. Unlike your puppets that lack organs, you must infuse the heart." Grave used his ax to lacerate Bryhan's chest.

Echo looked away, speaking aloud, "No hurt."

Grave explained, "He will not feel any physical harm in his condition, my Lord Foundling. You must provide blood. Come here," he extended his arcane ax, "I will cut your arm."

"No!" Sharon interceded, "There must be another way."

"You are a natural defender, Curator. But this he must do. The cost of necromancy requires that the caster donate what is dearest. It is fitting, Lord Echo, that you trade your puppets for a true minion. You can transfer your blood through them. In any event, this rite will end with a transformation. You will not get the puppets back."

Echo glanced at his dolls. He did not want to give these up, nor grow up. Yet he felt the time had come. His body changed faster than his mind, but the evidence was upon him. These figurines belonged to the Echo who had molted, not the Echo who stood here now. He gathered his dolls into a tight embrace, wishing them farewell and thanking them. Sharon rubbed his back as he sobbed. He said goodbye to the avian-wraith sister. And the ragdolls, soft as they were, had served him during an adolescent period in which he needed extra security. Dioramas and reenactments of the Ill Age's end need not be played anymore. Blood soaked the talismans. The rag figurines and the embryonic fowl were filled with the Gray Foundling's colorless ichor. Echo was then emotionally spent. He could not stand after this bloodletting. He slumped motionless.

Sharon took the three puppets and wrenched them over Lordson Bryhan's incision. Then she compressed them into Bryhan's chest. The white ichor sluiced into his body. Suddenly, the heart beat again. The transaction had sucked the dolls dry of substance. Fragile piles of ash soon replaced their forms.

"Such sorcery tires him. He will need energy, Curator Sharon. You must nurse him. Wrap him in the fabric, then draw on it." She did so. Her ink bladders emptied, aliquot by aliquot, as she peppered nightmares and hopes onto his canvas wrapped back: depictions of a vibrant Qual, a doting mother, an understanding father, and ballrooms filled with music. Yet the content mattered not, as long they were genuine. Her creativity fed the art, and the art fed her Lord. As hastily as she created, the art faded. This is how she healed her lord's spirit.

"Echo, Bryhan will protect you when he rises. He will be your Guard. Until then Curator Sharon will nurture you." Grave said.

Latent energy simmered inside the soldier, just like Echo's did. It would prove to be a slow process. Echo slept as Bryhan's corpse rejuvenated its arteries. Veins and vessels swelled with ichor, eventually. Both Lord and Guard rested.

THE LANTERN HAD been quenched to conserve oil. Doctor Grave and Echo could still *see*, so only Sharon sat in darkness. A day passed until subtle splashing was heard. Sharon asked, "What is going on, Lord Echo?"

"Bryhan stirs," the Gray Foundling said.

"Can we the light the lantern?" Sharon pleaded. Grave did so for her.

The resurrected Bryhan squatted, massaging his left shoulder, which lacked an arm. He looked curiously at his right hand with starlit eyes. He had died without that appendage, but somehow had regained it. His legs had also been repaired. He lived past death now, equipped with a rusted metal stanchion. Black liquid sluiced off slick, ivory scale mail. Bryhan's lamellar armor was made from serpent hide. Bran kneeled in obedience. "No arm?" Bran stared at the pole swinging over his mother's aura. "Why a spear, not my flail?" His voice was like that of a drowning man struggling to gasp for help as his throat filled.

The guttural speech terrified Sharon. She embraced Echo.

Doctor Grave spoke, "Son of Kaiyn. Welcome back."

Bryhan stirred.

"You ressurect me to be your slave?"

Grave clarified. "You now serve Lord Echo."

Aleece's ghost wavered from the spear before her Son. Bryhan spat, "You offer me with the weapon that once impaled my mother." He arose. "You? *You* impaled Aleece! You cut me to pieces!" With speed that belied a cripple, Bryhan speared the golem so fast that *Ferrus Hewnmaw* flew from the doctor's grip. Lifted aloft, Grave's head slammed into a stalactite. White ichor ran fast down the shaft.

Sharon gasped. Clumsily she held the lantern aloft. Its waning light barely revealed the scene.

"No... worries," Grave uttered, suspended. "I... lost... that battle. Now... I am controlled as you are. Undead, I serve Lord Protector Lysis, who animates me. You serve Echo, a Gray Lord. You are his servant now, Guard Bryhan. I... serve him too in my death. Do you recognize... him?"

"I know who he is. I named him," Guard Bryhan said. "Echo, I died for you. I died protecting you from... from... this demon!"

Echo was stunned into paralysis. He had given birth to a mighty warrior who exhibited strength beyond his own—perhaps greater than the Doctor's might!

Grave's blood ran down the shaft and mingled with that on the Guard's arms and chest. Eucrasiac blends of ichor were miscible and nontoxic, so no reaction occurred. "Lord Echo, the first task you must learn… is to… control your servant."

Guard Bryhan had no intention of lowering his nemesis.

Echo pleaded with his new minion telepathically: *"Bran, please. No more hurt. Let him down."*

Lordson Bryhan lowered his spear slowly, yet he did not remove it. Doctor Grave remained impaled, and thus constrained. Sharon did not see the tumultuous ether in which the ghost of Lady Aleece wrestled with the golem's aura. Invisible streams of energy crackled, seen only by the undead. The Doctor proved too mentally strong to yield to the astral attack. Likewise, his physical prowess was unmatched—the golem was clearly biding his time.

"It is not my blood that wets this spear," Grave said. "The blood of Lord Lysis fills my flesh and pumps my heart. I am the one who repaired your body. With Echo, I invited you back. I seek you no harm, Lordson Bryhan."

"A Lordson no longer!" Bryhan pressed with his forefoot onto the stanchion, so the Doctor was forced to squat. A right arm lashed out, smacking the Doctor's face such that it dented. Then five fingers dug into the clay neck until it seeped white drops.

A small hand touched the warrior's forearm. The boy's innocence quelled his anger. Echo's blood cooled inside him, and his heart quieted.

Guard Bryhan then kneeled, releasing his chokehold and grabbing the spear. The pink spirit of Aleece flared as it left the proximity of the golem. Bryhan spoke, "Lord Echo, I await your command."

Time slowed as Echo pondered. He looked at his two servants before him: Curator Sharon and Guard Bryhan. They needed his guidance, and yet his muses were not clear. They stood in a pool of ancient blood. Iron-rich, black melancholy. Oil dripped from a stalactite. Each splash amplified the passing of time.

Echo considered that he could not control his own powers, nor his servant, well. He had to get away. He had to go someplace that he could learn more about himself. "We go back to the Gallwomb."

Grave watched them leave.

For years after, the Gray Foundling would pursue his ambiguous visions—a quest that the Keepers would misinterpret as wanderlust. He would never enjoy baseless wandering, nor would he know exactly where he needed to travel. He knew only that his body changed every year and that he was compelled to find something that only he was meant to receive.

VIII: HELEN'S WISH

Ever since Sharon committed to living out her courtesan dreams with a reclusive, itinerant master, Helen had barely spoken to her. Ten years passed.

Helen cleaned piles of nutgalls in the Ink Hall. She had two baths: the first filled with a lye solution, and the second a vinegar wash. A trickling stream fell from the ceiling, splashing onto the filled cauldron of the former. Cold, bubbling wash-water overran onto the stone tile to seep between cracks into the Underworld. She immersed her arms in the vat of the soap bath to cleanse the gallnuts of dirt and debris. Well, she was *supposed* to be preparing them. Instead she played. Seven bushels awaited her attention. Opposite the baths sat several empty wheelbarrows ready to transfer material to those who would pulverize it.

Helen did not wear leather gloves like everyone else. She preferred to feel the textures of the galls, even if her skin became raw, prune-like, and slimy. Each nut was uniquely shaped, but they could be categorized into groups based on which insect spawned it. The most abundant was the oak-apple variety. These were pale green spheres the size of fingertips, birthed in the spring when gallflies impregnated oak stems about the southern Chromlechon. They fell onto the ground the following year to be harvested. Other types were smaller, like red berries, or larger with spikey tumors. Helen adored these natural relics. Infestations could manifest into grotesque sights, like necrophagous wasps burrowing into corpses; or they could produce symmetric ornaments of great beauty like these galls. These shapes were worth feeling, admiring, Helen reflected. Insects created beauty sometimes, so there was hope for all affected, directly or indirectly, by dyscrasia.

The soap bath bubbled under the trickling waterfall. Some galls floated while others sank. Several sought to escape yet could not overcome the rim. Helen was likewise trapped. She was essentially confined to the Chromlechon, yet wanted to be away from the Keepers. Helen sought Sharon out as often as possible, but her friend ventured much more often than she visited. When Sharon did return, she was still difficult to find. Sharon tried to keep everyone, Helen included, away from Echo.

Helen had no other friends here. She often sought solace in the tunnels below the Chromlechon, the deep reaches of earth and Ill Age ruins that only Doctor Grave seemed familiar with. If only she could be exploring now.

The rhythmic hammering of dried galls echoed in the vaulted workshop. All the other initiate curators toiled away, uniformed in waxen aprons over plain shifts. None of the two dozen in the Ink Hall resembled, nor understood, Helen. They ignored her when possible.

Frayed Angie still covered Helen's shoulders. The aged hide showed its years of wear. It was more of a knotted skein than a cohesive pelt. Helen could never remember what dress she was supposed to wear for any given task or ritual. In fact, she took to *not* wearing shifts since they were confining. Doctor Grave ensured all Keepers wielded flags anyway, and Helen decided to just wrap herself in the ceremonial pennant instead of carrying the cumbersome staff. Everyone had to craft for the Pyre now, and all carried ink bladders on their belts. Helen did conform this way, since she enjoyed drawing and it was useful to have dyes ready.

"Ahem." Two yards away, a Keeper wielding a hammer addressed Helen. Pigface, as Helen referred to him in her mind, was awkwardly surviving adolescence. His cheeks were puffy and marked with ripe pimples. The fellow peered under a lowered brow with an open palm extending toward the empty carts. Piggy and Horsehead, his friend from Tonn, would need more galls to crush.

Helen plucked one oak-apple out of the bath, and offered it. Flickering lamplight did little to illuminate the wet sphere as it shed dark drops onto the cold floor.

Pigface did not accept this, turning his nose away from her curly, unkempt nails. "You're goin' to slow the whole line down if ya don't do ya' job." He snorted before returning to his workstation. Piggy worked with the wide-nostrilled Horseface on their last pile. After they smashed the galls, they treated the powder in boiling sulfate baths. Water would simmer off. Resulting brown slurries slowly turned into black ink. Once cooled, the ink was filtered and funneled into pig bladders, horns, and small jars at the opposite end of the Ink Hall.

Alone in the corner, she rummaged through the bushels of iron-galls. The larger green ones she set into the soap pot. Granted, the Ink Hall was not all terrible. She usually enjoyed the pseudo-anonymity by being stationed away from the groups. Pungent wafts of lye and vinegar drifted over the churning cauldrons. The smell reminded her of her father's beamhouse.

Best get productive, Helen figured, *else Piggy will risk speaking to me again.* Hastily, she transferred the contents of the soap pot to the vinegar wash. Then, with a small knife, she scraped away stems and leaves and refilled the first station. Water continued to flow from above to below.

Helen paused again to contemplate, twirling the ribbon in her hair. The crowds of Keepers drained her. She felt more at peace being by herself, rooting through the earth where social interactions were rare. There were still plenty of ruins to explore apart from the buzzing masses. An entire city lay buried under volcanic ash nearby, and countless tunnels, plumbed by elder insects, formed a network through the entire mountain. Helen often walked the abandoned ruins of the old-Chromlechon, the streets devoid of humans, a snapshot of the past hidden beneath everyone's feet. She was never entirely alone since Lysis's Pyre sprites kept her company, but she was away from the Keepers. If only Helen was there now, avoiding their judgement.

The blood-plague that took centuries to fester would take at least decades to cleanse. It was *not* enough time for the Land to be made safe from dyscrasiac gargoyles, but the city of orphans had matured into young adults. Still, the Keepers were human and exhibited all the frailties one would expect. Many repressed memories, forgot names, and immersed themselves in developing the new culture. All had roles to keep, like farming. Apple and pear orchards grew plentiful on the south side of the mountain, as did wheat, so the boundaries of the Keep expanded to include verdant highlands. Oak trees adjacent to the fruit were inundated with gallflies, and thus infected and spurred the making of galls. Waterfalls powered two mills that reduced grain and transformed grass into fibers to produce paper.

Most Keepers did not venture far. Only the Gray Lords led expeditions beyond the Blood Bogs and Gray Orchard. Lysis hunted while Echo fulfilled some cryptic personal mission. Only select servants who had received long-term tutelage under Doctor Grave attended these sorties. The Lords' returns were marked with fanfare atop South Gate. Keepers were expected to cease their chores to welcome them, especially the initiate nurses.

The surface of the soap pot rippled. Drowned flies emerged in grotesque clusters. Some were wiggling larvae, others more mature. This happened on occasion. Sometimes the galls were harvested before the gallflies could get out. Each was an egg after all. Helen procured a ladle to skim the floaters.

A swarm of flies formed above the dry bushels. Never

had she seen such masses. She swatted them with her ladle. *Clang!* She lashed through the living cloud, striking the metal cauldron. The Ink Hall workers glanced, saw that it was only Helen acting strangely, and continued their work.

She looked at the piles of leafy nutgalls. They moved as if some rodent was attempting to unearth itself. Swatting did little to thin the cloud of flies. Spitting, she expelled a mouthful. Peering into the barrel again, she did not see the expected galls, but hundreds of little faces and thin limbs, instead. Miniature, bodiless puppet-heads stared at her from under the water. Out of their gaping lips maggots squirmed.

She closed her eyes, counted to three, and opened them to confirm the vision. They were merely dirty galls again. Yet the flies still flew thicker than usual. Many landed on her pale arms.

Helen gasped, then cowered.

She decided to leave the infestation for a time. She hurriedly collected the cleaned galls from the vinegar wash with a strainer, and emptied these into a cart. Flies obscured her path to the hammer men. The insects began to hover around Pigface and Horsehead. Some landed on their foreheads, even burrowed into Horsehead's enflamed nostrils. The young men did not seem bothered. They never slowed their work, yet they noted her standing there longer than usual.

Helen scratched the air to shoo the gallflies away.

The two peered suspiciously as they received the clean galls.

Helen observed Pigface's cheeks ripple. The gallflies

were laying eggs in his skin! His pimples swelled into fruit-like galls. Then they spread to Horsehead. The insects deposit their eggs into them! *Those boys are not trees, stupid flies.* Her eyes dilated as she stared in horror at the dangling clusters of red orbs. She motioned with her hands outstretched to pluck them away. She reached out her scrawny arms and extended her dripping fingers.

"Why are y' flailin'. What's y'r problem?"

"Careful, she's ill. She may be contagious," warned Horsehead.

"Get back to work." Piggy pushed her away.

Helen stumbled back, and fell to the ground. The swarm descended on her. She felt them rooting into her skin. Brushing them away did not prevent the masses from infesting her. Pustules formed where larvae were implanted. Her nails clawed at them. She wrestled against the shadows, rolling on the wet ground.

Pigface watched her seizure.

"Just avoid her. We have enough to work with for now." Horsehead added, "If she don't recover by the day's end, we'll get Doc'."

"He may lock her up this time," Piggy laughed.

Helen looked up from the floor. Clouds of flies obscured her vision. The rhythmic hammering started again. She struggled to rise. Dizziness poisoned her balance. She clamped onto Angie hoping to extract some power. Then…

Bonnggg! A handheld gong sounded from the entrance to the Ink Hall. The crier, a red capped young boy, had come to inform all: "Doctor Grave says that both Lords come back now. Hurry, we must welcome them."

The Inkers switched tasks. Except for Helen, they tidied up their workstations, hung their aprons, and gathered their pennants and their ink bladders. A line of initiate nurses formed a parade behind the boy with his censer and gong. Over twenty exited, walking in an orderly manner with their flags. Grave had taught them all that creativity fueled the Lords' sorcery, but they could only imagine the streams of ether connecting Pyre to sprite, nurse to flag, and all to the lords. Like the other initiates, Helen had her own flag to practice the arts of nursing. Of course, she wore it now instead of the standard shift.

Two young men remained behind wondering about what to do with Helen.

"Look, she ain't even wearin' proper clothes."

Horsehead spat, "She never is. She just wraps herself in that mangy pelt. And is that her flag? Is she naked besides that?"

"Let us wake 'r." Pigface suggested.

"Get y'r gloves back on if ya gonna touch her."

A bucket of soap water splashed Helen's face. She wheezed for air. The assault did set the flies back. Helen was angry, yet almost grateful. Were they helping her?

"That cleaned her up a bit. Do it again."

Mucus clogged Helen's nose. She stood on shaky legs. Retreating clumsily into the bushel, she toppled backward. A cascade of gallnuts spilled out. Helen saw the pair as an encroaching, two-headed wraith. She fell. The prickly embrace of a thousand sticks welcomed her and exhaled haunting memories into her lungs. She coughed.

"Sharon!" She cried out to an invisible phantom.

They ignored her. "What's 'n her hair? It's a rat nest."

Another dose of water struck her.

Blinded by the wash, Helen was surprised when her hair was abruptly tugged. Cold air frosted her bare shoulders as Angie was ripped from her back. Before she could yell, her head was dunked into the soap cauldron. Her eyes stung with lye as she stared into the eyes of doll heads. They came alive, butted against her face, nibbled at her. Again, her hair tugged.

Piggy and Horsehead scrubbed her forcefully.

"Get a new shift. This one is ruined," a muffled voice commanded.

"Beware the bugs!" she spat, arching her back. Why were they not concerned about the gallflies? "Stop holding me. We must run away!"

"Ya need to dress, woman! Ya there. I am speakin' to ya." A strange hand clamped Helen's jaw, and turned her head so they looked eye to eye.

She looked into the empty sockets of an avian skull, a wraith's skull decorated with red galls. Its mandibles opened. Hot fetid breath roiled out to suffocate her.

Helen screamed.

Her mouth was covered in haste. She could not breathe. Desperately, she bit down and tasted only leather. Hyperventilating, she wriggled uncontrollably. Alien appendages held her down. They pressed into her back, held her elbows, knees, and shoulders—all joints were anchored. The cobblestone under her grew hot. Steamed roiled across the floor. Her Da's beamhouse was burning. She had to get out…

Another bucket of water doused the fire. Made her cold again. She remained pressed against a carpet of dead flies and broken galls. Adrenaline fueled her escape.

Helen sprang to her feet, shoved Pigface so that he collided into Horsehead, and darted out of the Ink Hall. She did not know which direction she fled, initially. She quickly found herself lodged in a congested corridor of flag-bearing Keepers. Interrupting the parade, she squeezed between person and hewn wall, shoving and pressing until she emerged into a side corridor.

She descended a level of the Chromlechon. Sparse torchlight from sconces guided her. Clacking footsteps followed. No doubt, Keepers ran after her. Lower and lower she went. Away from them all.

Helen's wet skin only chilled as she descended into the mines. With each step the shadows grew and spilled over the cracks and crevices. Darker and darker her path became, until she shot into a large cavern, as evidenced by the echoing of her steps. Twinkling reflections from curvaceous stalagmites lit her way. It was as if she had stepped into a celestial forest, the undergrowth full of sparkling ferns and crystal fronds. Scarce men swung picks to harvest gypsum flowers. Boys covered with powdered jewels stood to attention as she bolted. She ran past the ghostly visages as fast she could. Helen was like a screaming comet.

Footsteps echoed in the chamber and Helen's mind. The distance between the pursuers and herself was impossible to assess. She kept running.

Through this chamber and down the next. Her journey became darker and colder still.

Helen's mind battled her rage and managed to set her direction now. Ahead was the Red Teeth caverns, and beyond that her logical goal. She was beneath the Blood Bogs presently, which dripped its black liquor through earthen cracks, trickling with water through limestone and battlefield-residues. More miners were here collecting iron-rich minerals from stalactite and stalagmite. Their lanterns cast warm, yellow light onto these colossal, red teeth. That ceiling never ceased weeping. She stomped through puddles of the melancholic liquid. She was watched by warped effigies of humans roosting atop the dendritic rock formations. Dreamy gargoyles, sentries of the Underworld, glared. Several miners reached out to her, followed her. They shouted unintelligible warnings. She ran faster. Deeper she ran, navigating the enormous rusty teeth, running headlong toward the wet jowls of the Underworld's mouth.

At last, her destination approached. Beyond the Red Teeth, through the dragon's mouth, Doctor Grave and Lord Lysis were known to take the creatures they found abroad.

Helen entered the yawning throat. Pungent smells that were most foul affronted her: excrement, salty sweat, and acrid bile. Helen doubled over to vomit. Behind her, silhouettes of confused Keepers muddled within dimming light. They refused to follow her. She crawled forward. Chilling safety enveloped her.

Gloom fell upon her, comforting her in darkness.

She was free.

Elated, she found a crawlspace to settle in, and immersed herself in the peaceful isolation. Continuous drafts indicated a wide canyon spread before her, even though she could not see it. Licking blood off her nails, she passed some time. Her eyes finally adjusted. She struggled to discern the dungeon.

Suspended over an ocean of emptiness were dozens of gibbets. Glowing blue eyes hovered two fathoms away. Within the cages she saw avian-insectan-human hybrids, some animated, some still. Many were dominantly human with bloated buboes—many were mere children. Others were entirely inhuman, with wings and horns. All had magical, diseased ichor that glowed through their veins and eyes.

Not all were imprisoned as individuals. Several pairs coexisted in shared cages. Opposite genders, forced to remain together. Was this a zoological collection of dyscrasiac beasts, or an infirmary for those with terminal illness? One set contained three large, insectan babies. These dead infants looked familiar.

None of the Keepers would chase her here. Only fools would come here.

"FEW COME TO my dungeon for respite." Grave looked down at Helen. Several glowing sprites perched on her shoulders, limning her with a warm corona.

"The others would not follow me here."

"Indeed, most of the Keepers went to South Gate to welcome the Gray Lords, who have yet to arrive. But before they left, several cleaned these for you." The Doctor offered her washed pelt and flag. Then he passed along a set of three ink-bladders. Angie was still wet, but Helen covered her shoulders anyway. Grave watched her aura grow as they reconnected. "I also brought an apple, figuring you would be hungry."

Helen took the fruit but did not eat it. She cupped it in her hands marveling at its smooth skin. Two sprites inspected it.

"You look afraid." The Doctor said. She was not as bloody as her thoughts depicted. What had the Keepers done to her? Did they actually hurt her? "The others only meant to change you into someone like themselves."

"They attacked me."

The Doctor noted her sharp, bloodied fingernails. The bleeding was limited, but her exposed, red blood glowed brilliantly. Had she scratched herself? "Humans are imperfect. The Keepers are scared that you may bring them harm."

"Why?"

"You see beauty when they see revulsion. You see the horrors that they want to forget. You interpret their kindness as malice."

She assented. "I'm backward. Should I leave the Keep?"

"And risk becoming those in my cages?"

Helen was confused. "They are not your patients?"

Grave laughed. "No, they are my prisoners. Many are

outright creatures, caught by Lysis. Dead or alive, I cage them. Though some are orphans who never sought sanctuary and became ill. They are threatened not only from brutal attacks, but from impregnation too. Understand, the dyscrasiac cannot mate with their own kind, so they try to mate with healthy humans. The gargoyles do more than kill. They also seek to impregnate victims in strange ways. Like the flesh-galls on that one. Each bubo is an egg. If they hatch, the larvae may feed on him."

Helen surveyed the gibbets. "What happens if they mate?"

Doctor Grave pointed toward a cage with statue of two couple creatures. "It depends. They often turn to stone. Some mutate. Offspring never survive."

"Why do you keep them alive?"

"I study them for a cure."

"You experiment with them?" Her brows shifted and eyes dilated to tease out details from the dark. "What if they get out?"

"They would fall to their deaths. Some have. You know… this dungeon of *mine* is not for young women."

"For me, the upper levels are more dangerous." Helen considered. "Where can I escape to, if I do not belong with the other Keepers, nor your dungeon?"

"Helen, your personal strength, and weakness, is that you interpret reality differently than most." Grave advised. "I will guide you away from here." He led her away from his dungeon.

Helen asked as she followed, "So what is wrong with

me? Can you heal me?"

"You do *not* need a doctor. Your muse leads you into trouble. We each have one."

"You too?"

Grave's eye's flared. "My muse, the spirit in my blood, is concerned with family. And obedience."

"Mine?"

The doctor examined her aura. Angie's ethereal presence cocked its head as if listening. "Your muse... is yours to discover. Do you remember the doctrines describing Muses and Blood?"

Helen recalled the Doctor's training in the Theater. "Well, there is the 'Rule of Muses' in which 'Artists are inspired by the emotive ether. As they craft, they consume that which ignited their creativity.' And there is the Rule of Blood and Ether," she paused to recollect, "... in which 'Blood is the medium between the physical world with the ethereal, connecting soul to body.' See, I can recite the rules." Helen kicked a pebble. "I am just not sure how to apply them."

"Application is the most challenging, and rewarding. You need only obey your muse."

"My muse is difficult to follow."

"No need to catch what is already in your blood," Grave laughed. "Muses already have hold of you. Your quest is not to find it, but to go where it compels you."

"So, I am being pushed?"

Grave did not answer this time. They ascended again but not through the gypsum flower cavern. He took her to isolated ruins, the old Chromlechon city. The sprites remained on Helen's shoulders.

"I know these old passages are no secret to you. Let us go to the main street."

Helen walked side by side with the Doctor except when rocks intervened. Thrice they alternated taking the lead, strafing between rubble, and climbing stairways both natural and artificial. Eventually, scarce sunbeams illuminated a corridor, breaching the arched ceiling of volcanic ash. Despite the sunlight, shadows prevailed on the circuitous path. Collapsed architecture melded with sandstone boulders and ashen sculptures. The Doctor set up his Theater to study death, which was plentiful prior to the breaking of Cypria's Gallwomb. Skeletons lay where their owners had come out of their market stands to gaze upon a divine event that shot wonderful colors across the sky. The beauty they had beheld had been overcome by a trailing storm of molten earth.

"What do you want to do here?" Helen asked, stopping to inspect a pile of bird carcasses. She bent down, sitting beside it to rest. She rotated the apple in her hand.

"Well, I wanted you to get out of the dungeon. I'll need to attend South Gate soon and this path leads me there." Grave reflected as she cringed. "You need not accompany me. Continue to your favorite lookout. Yes, I know your secret places, but do not worry. No one will find you there, and your absence will be sanctioned."

"What are you looking at?" Helen expanded the wings of a dead pigeon.

The Doctor snickered for he had been caught analyzing her aura. "You are an enigma. You fear inanimate oak galls, but are un-phased with bird carcasses."

Helen shrugged.

"Let me attempt to guide you. I will tell you a short fable of pigeons and blackbirds. In the city, pigeons and blackbirds flock in search of food. The pigeons navigate the feet of trafficking humans, frantically snatching crumbs left between busy feet. The pigeons trail the people, eating fresh scraps of meat. They fill their bellies and wonder why the blackbirds are so timid, waiting hungrily for the humans to leave before feasting. One pigeon professed, 'How foolish for the fearful blackbirds to wait?' And the other, who wished not to share, replied, 'How good for us!'"

She imagined the skeletons alive again, pecking the ground.

Grave continued. "At night, when the humans retired and streets quieted, the blackbirds feasted on the scraps of *roasted* pigeon. One said, 'I dreamt all day of eating this fat pigeon.' And his cohort replied, 'How foolish to follow the feet of the person who would eventually cook it?' The pigeon was blind to its own callings, distracted from life by its killer's trash. And the first blackbird said, 'How fortunate for us!'"

Helen poked the lifeless birds. "I don't understand the fortunate part. All the birds died anyway."

"Foolish of me to clarify your calling, though you should know that death escapes many souls. You tell me. Where does your muse take you? What do you wish to become?" She was not prepared to answer, and he was not ready to listen since his focus shifted to receive a telepathic message. "Ah, it is time. I must go. Our lords return." Helen remained sitting as the Doctor began to depart. At last he said, "You too should watch the procession. Go to your lookout, contemplate your muse."

HELEN ROTATED HER canvas sash to protect the attached ink bladders, then lay on her stomach to peer outward from the mountain. She carefully held the apple in her left hand. Sunlight poured onto her cheeks, making her squint, as her legs remained in the cave's cool recess. She pushed aside the two jagged-edged leaves with her tongue to bite into the crisp fruit, its polished skin fracturing to release sweet nectar down her lip. A tangy, sweet burst of fragrance plumed, opening her nostrils.

The scores of radiant sprites that escorted Helen's journey through the Chromlechon's core swooped down onto her shoulders. They always joined her in watching the spectacle of the returning lords. Lysis's enflamed, paper minions assumed many guises. Winged chimera stalked her back, rooted through her lengthy, ivory hair. The embers on each fold brightened with the open air. A sphinx with gilded wings roosted atop the silk ribbon given to her by Sharon. Apparently jealous of the position, a six-legged-fawn and a tailed-arachnid playfully battled for a seat beside the sphinx. Each was about the size of an adult mantis and represented a hope, or nightmare, of a different Keeper. The three minions nestled on the ribbon. Auras blended. Energy amplified, flared, to scorch Helen's pelt. She did not mind the occasional burning—that is, until enough congregated and puffs of smoke alerted her to fire. She then swooshed them away with a flick of her hand.

Helen's eyes were wide and ready to catch a glimpse of Sharon. Helen was very proud of her. On occasion, Sharon had time to speak of her adventures. The treks were scary. She confirmed that the Land was still plagued with dyscrasiac monsters, and begged Helen to stay inside the Keep. Echo had to search abroad trying to learn about himself while Lysis hunted down creatures. Still, Sharon loved her role as dutiful servant, as perilous as it may be. Ironically, Echo was feared by the Keepers since he mysteriously kept to himself and assumed inhuman qualities; he seemed to be transforming into the type of creature that Lysis would hunt. Sharon and the Gray Foundling were essentially shunned. Sharon said it was safer for everyone that way. Even Echo was not confident in his ability to control his feeding of color. So, Echo kept his distance.

Helen offered Sharon the opportunity to serve Echo too. But this was declined outright. *'He abhors endangering me, but Doctor Grave insisted he take at least one Curator. Lord Echo would never allow you to be close to him, nor leave on the dangerous missions.'* Sharon explained. She had even come to tears many times, unable to explain the horrors she faced. When pressed for details, she had replied, *"I've seen outsiders. They live with constant fear and hunger. Stay in the Keep!"* Helen then begged Sharon to stay away from Echo. Why continue to do something so dangerous? Sharon explained that serving a Lord had been her childhood dream and that Echo was good natured. He was just cursed with a dark muse.

Helen had to steal glances of Sharon from afar. Presently, she licked the juices streaming down her fingers, maintaining her vigil. She ate meticulously. In fact, she sculpted more than ate. The core was exposed. She was careful to eat around it while she shaped it into being. The rounded fruit now appeared as a butterfly with the two leaves becoming angelic wings.

This niche peered out from the vertical side of north-eastern cliff of the Chromlechon. Her lookout held one of her many hidden stashes. This ossuary had Sharon's tooth amongst fossilized oddities of unknown age and origin. On previous nights, aided by the light of full moons, Helen watched the ashen fog lift from Qual. Each year, the miasma retracted incrementally. Hardly any remained. Lord Lysis and his retinue patrolled the Land monthly to cleanse the scourge. Each sortie, it seemed, promised the end of blue-blooded gargoyles. Yet they always resurfaced enough to reinforce the need to stay inside. The haunted fog was not missed, but its absence only exposed wrecked civilization. She recalled those haunted grounds from a decade ago. Now the land was exposed to view from miles away, but it remained as lifeless. Little grew atop the swathes of ash. Desiccated, limbless tree trunks still dominated any new vegetation. As much as Helen mourned her family, and missed her home, she knew her future was not to be played out there on the outskirts of the clanhold once known as Qual.

Helen spied over the Gorgepath from the soaring,

cavernous nook. First came Lord Lysis with a grand retinue. Then, after the fanfare calmed, Lord Echo would return—usually taller than he had left. A late afternoon sun splashed orange-purple shades onto the columns of prancing ants. Reverberations tunneled up through the rock. The rumbling sounds reminded her of Sharon's wagon approaching her homestead. The columns came from the eastern clan of Tonn, through the Gray Orchard, over the causeway splicing the blood bogs, and over hills of scree. Lysis sauntered ahead atop the tusked once-Queen. Behind him came his band of nurses, Curators, holding flags while they rode her reanimated soldiers. Their pennants were more than standards, for they were the tools of sorcery. Upon these canvases they offered paintings. These depictions were drained of color and form, their master empowered and healed during his missions. Cecelia headed Lysis's nurses. She had traded her striped socks in for a standard white shift, and her pigtails replaced with a single braid. Helen sensed that Cecelia had lost any sense of being a child.

This sortie had won the retinue five carcasses and three living specimens. All were blue-blooded gargoyles. Soldier ants carried the ghastly corpses upon their backs. Manacles and ropes restrained the injured mutants. Ill ichor spilled from fractured chitin, wounds delivered by *Ferrus Eviscamir,* sparkling like molten sapphire under the cold twilight. Some of these avian-insectan-human hybrids would grace the Gray Orchard soon. Others, Doctor Grave would lock in his dungeon, then employ the bodies in demonstrations to teach nurses. This is how Helen would learn the ways of alchemy, pyromancy, and geomancy.

The sun sank faster and deeper behind the Chromlechon. Lysis's train entered the Keep in evening shadow. Helen listened to the retinue enter the South Gate above her, cheered by the young ones, mere children birthed by orphans. The Keepers would not receive Lord Echo's band with this enthusiasm.

The sprites repositioned themselves, buzzing about Helen's head.

"There's Sharon!" Helen indicated. From the west, Sharon came forth riding the back of her Lord, bearing a canvas standard. Her hair glistened with flames of coppery fire as the sun's rays infiltrated just right. The spear-totting Guard Bryhan was there too, riding an eldritch soldier. Sharon still had Lacey attached to her belt; she peered toward the cliff where she knew Helen would be watching. Helen smiled. That short gesture was enough to sustain their friendship. The Foundling Lord had grown in increments each year, and was now taller than his lone, undead guard. Echo had even sprouted an extra set of legs. According to Sharon, Echo forgot much of his past with each molting. The Lord became more and more solitary as he appeared less and less human. His mutating into a mantis-human scared the other Keepers, but not Helen. She saw things differently, and knew from her friend that he was not evil. Echo was a victim like all the other orphans who ended up in the Keep. His ancestors were different, not his circumstances. He sought purpose in a strange world with little guidance and much peril.

Helen felt different from the Keepers, of course. She did miss being with her best friend, but, in her heart, she was

happy because her friend's wish had come true. Sharon was a
true courtesan to a lord. When it came to wishes, Helen was a
believer.

Grave had taught Helen that flags were not a necessary
medium for transferring creativity. Any artifact could suffice.
She beheld the denuded apple, now shaped as a glossy caterpil-
lar. Two seeds of the fruit's five were placed as eyes on the
figurine's head; the last three formed a line on the anterior.
Helen pricked her bladder of black ink. She used her curved
nails as quills to draw miniature icons of Sharon's Lacey on
the right wing, and of Angie on the left. Space allowed only for
coarse, stick-figure representations. The apple doll was thus tat-
tooed. Finally, she encouraged the enflamed sprites to hug her
offering. They crawled forth, embracing the carven butterfly
until creamy *lapis elixir* leaked from the animated cluster onto
the still one. As the sprites withdrew, Lysis's ichor remained
behind. The offering's wings smoldered as the original Pyre-
born stepped back. Properly imbibed, the apple's soul ignited.
The small stem split and transmuted to antennae, which became
pliable like its backbone.

"I maintain my wish." Helen cupped her apple creation
in her hands. The sprites lined up on her forearms. She inhaled
until her cheeks reddened. With a puff, she sent her message
fluttering away. The lighted sprites followed out the mountain.
Plumes of embers trailed. Their bodies remained bright, sail-
ing the winds like mini lanterns as they descended into the
Gorgepath.

"Go friends." One day Helen's wish would come true.

That was for certain. "I will join you someday. Not as a pigeon, nor blackbird, nor human. But as a magical fairy."

That day would be another nine years in the future, nearly twenty years since she had arrived at the Chromlechon. By then, all the Keepers, save Helen, would forget who Sharon was. In fact, even though Helen would stay in the Keep for the duration, the Keepers would continue to avoid her. Lysis had heard her wish many times over the years. As a sorcerer of the creative arts, he recognized her nascent power via his minions. He had marked her ever since her cat-spirt saved him from Lady Sabina's crypt. It was clear that Helen held more potential than his retinue of orderly Curators. Lord Lysis, Gray Lord Protector, would keep an eye on her until the time was right to deliver her wish. One day, she would hone her ability to create and to *see* as the undead do. Her transformation into a sorceress was as inevitable, as was Echo morphing into his final, terrifying imago…

ILL AGE: LORDS OF DYSCRASIA

What happened during the Ill Age when dyscrasia plagued the land? Read Lysis's transformation from a human into a demi-god in *Lords of Dyscrasia* (or listen to via Audible narrated by Thomas B. Hackett)!

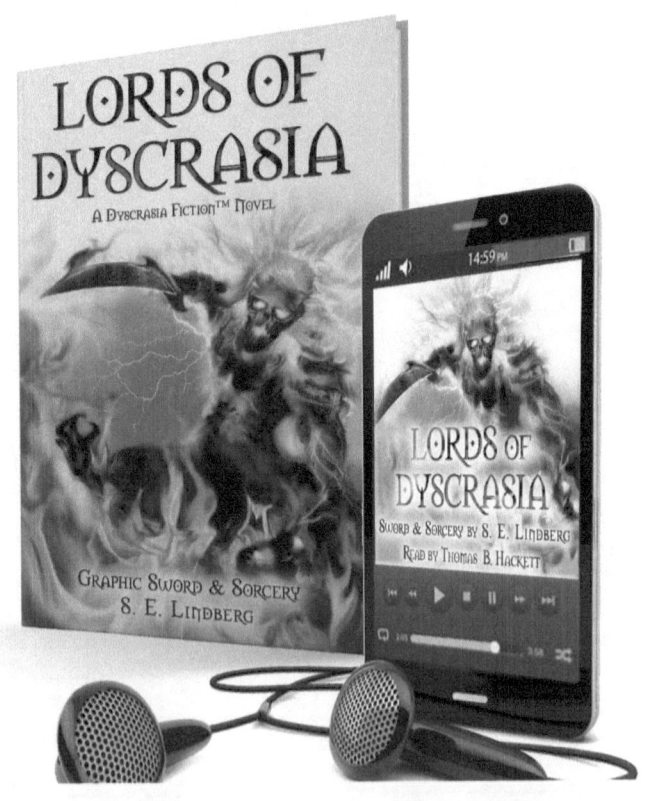

HELEN'S FATE: SPAWN OF DYSCRASIA

What will happen to Helen and Sharon as the roots of dyscrasia are revealed? Read *Spawn of Dyscrasia* to find out (or listen to via Audible narrated by Kathy Bell Denton)!

About the Author

8.E. Lindberg resides near Cincinnati, Ohio working as a microscopist, employing his skills as a scientist and artist to understand the manufacturing of products analogous to medieval paints. Two decades of practicing chemistry, combined with a passion for the Sword & Sorcery genre, spurred him to write graphic adventure fictionalizing the alchemical humors in Dyscrasia Fiction ®.

Connect with him *via his blog* in which he explores "Beauty in Weird Fiction" or the Sword & Sorcery group which he *co-moderates on Goodreads.com.*

If you are interested in alchemy-inspired into heroic fiction, please follow the developing Dyscrasia Fiction series and Perseid Press anthologies, Heroika.

HEROIKA: THE BIRTH OF ALCHEMICAL WARFARE

Heroika 1: Dragon Eaters, the first in an emerging historical-fantasy series from Perseid Press, showcases seventeen perspectives on killing serpents from ancient to modern times. The forthcoming second installment, *Heroika 2: Shieldless,* likewise fuses mythological themes with adventure, this time by tracking unarmored heroes & skirmishers across time.

"Legacy of the Great Dragon," S.E. Lindberg's short story for *Heroika 1: Dragon Eaters,* features the Father of Alchemy Thoth (a.k.a. Hermes) entombing his singular source of magic, the Great Dragon. According to Greek and Egyptian myth, Hermes was able to see into the world of the dead and pass his teachings to the living. One of the earliest known hermetic scripts is the Divine Pymander of Hermes Mercurius Trismegistus. Within that, a tale is told of Hermes being confronted with a vision of the otherworldly entity Pymander, who takes the shape of a "Great Dragon" to reveal divine secrets. "Legacy of the Great Dragon" fictionalizes this Hermetic Tradition, presenting the

Great Dragon as the sun-eating Apep of Egyptian antiquity. Hermes's teachings are passed to humanity via an Emerald Tablet.

The actual Emerald Tablet (if it was indeed "real") is arguably the most popular work of Hermeticism since it reveals the secret of transmuting any material's base elements into something divine or valuable (gold). Many refer to the Tablet as being the philosopher's stone, or the knowledge embodying it. In fact, the tablet no longer physically exists, but translations of it do. Sir Isaac Newton's translation of the tablet's inscription remains very popular, and undeniably cryptic.

Following the Emerald Tablet from Ancient Egypt into the Hellenistic age, the "The Naked Daemon" entry in Heroika 2 pits the mystic Apollonius of Tyana (deceased ~100 CE) against zealots who destroy what remains of the Alexandria Library. In life, his principles had been aligned with those of the pacifist gymnosophists (a.k.a. naked philosophers); hundreds of years past his death, Apollonius finds himself reborn as a daemon empowered with Hermes's Emerald Tablet. He observes the Roman oppression over pagan scholars and is challenged with an urgent need to defend knowledge. Will he rationalize war by unleashing the power of alchemy to do harm? Will he become an angel or demon? How will alchemy transform The Naked Demon?